NEST

The River Bend Series

TJ MAKKAI

This book is a work of fiction. The characters, events, and storyline are drawn from the author's imagination and are not to be construed as real. Any resemblance to actual persons, living or dead, businesses, companies, or events is entirely coincidental.

For information contact:
Email: info@makkaibooks.com
Website: www.tjmakkai.com

Editing: Starr Baumann with Quiethouse Editing
Cover: Jason Van Winkle
Formatting: Bad Doggie Designs

ISBN: 979-8-9894414-9-5

BOOKS BY TJ MAKKAI

The River Bend Series
In Order
CROW
HAWK
PIGEON
SPARROW
THE NEST

Their Confessions and My Lies
Coming up next: *Their Stories and My Lies*

I dedicate this to Wanderlust.
(My EARLs)

Helen, Ernessa, Molly,
Linda, Jill, Mary, Alexis,
Kelly, Mel, Jen, Krissy

Our adventures to the mountains, flatlands, oceans, and
rivers, and everywhere in between
bring me joy and renew my inner spirit.

Thank you for always saying yes.

PART 1

CHAPTER ONE

I'd been sitting on the porch for so long I didn't know what day it was. My thumb was numb from flicking the dollar gas-station lighter. At that point, I didn't know what would last longer, the butane fuel in the lighter or my urge to set the makeshift Goodwill-bedsheet curtains on fire. I wouldn't even have to hold the lighter to the curtains. Just flick it and let the wind do the rest.

The secrets buried in this house had shifted my core beliefs and the meaning of home. The only thing stopping me was someone might be in the house. I shouldn't assume they could get out. I didn't have the energy or soul to warn them.

People have stopped coming over to grieve with me and have most definitely stopped asking if I needed anything. Out of understanding the need for isolation, I stopped suggesting they check on Pete's family. I no longer had the energy to fend off those that were saying they were there to support me, but instead, I ended up consoling them.

My family and friends had been keeping me semi-fed, semi-clean, and semi-coherent. Not for lack of trying on their part, I had limited capacity to accept anything above the bare minimum to exist. The hollow, endless pit in me was at odds with my spinning mind. My family and friends took shifts on who was responsible for me. I couldn't tell you who was in the house now, but the sounds differed from the last time I thought outside of this particular chapter.

At the funeral, one of the nameless supporters said something about this chapter in my life. There were many more words, but it was that one word, *chapter*, that swirled in my head, and then my heart dropped.

I didn't want a chapter with Pete. I wanted the whole damn book of Claudia and Pete.

CHAPTER TWO

Months Prior.

I love those moments when you're having an ordinary but good day and then something gobsmacks you, and everything shifts. It was a Tuesday, I mean what extraordinary things happen on a Tuesday in March?

After a ten-and-half-hour shift at the hotel, I was done with work and people.

I texted my roommates, my friend Sherrie and my Aunt EG:

> Me: Hungry? What do you all have a
> craving for?
> Sherrie: No dinner for me but I will
> bring back dessert.

EG: I got us pizza. Just need beer or
something fun to drink.
Sherrie: Claud - Don't forget boxes.

Sherrie, one of my former college roommates, and I had been living with EG, since we'd graduated from college two years ago. Sherrie was in the midst of her master's program and would gear up for her doctoral program in psychology, social work, or something else that helps people. I should really have know this by now. Weirdly, about a month ago, Sherrie started bringing home empty boxes. After accepting EG's invite to live with us, Sherrie moved into EG's old office.

EG was a highly successful mystery writer and was an occasional college professor. For several decades, EG had collected books and research material having to do with crime scene investigations, FBI and police procedures, and medical books. These days, you could find all the stuff online, and most of those books were outdated. EG just had never gotten around to getting rid of the old materials and told Sherrie to dump it when she moved in. Sherrie's room was double the size of a regular room, and she just pushed the old materials out of the way. Now something must have prompted her to finally get rid of it after two years.

The other weird thing since living with EG was not living with EG. She had a condo in Chicago where she spent most of her time when not traveling. Between writing books, EG taught writing at Jameson College and spearheaded the book club at the local high school. Again, this fall, for the third semester in a row, she had opted out of teaching her writing seminar. She did spend a whole two weeks here last October. Other than that, it hadn't been more than three days at a time in River Bend.

The first year we lived with her, she was all about exploring the world on cruise ships. She soon discovered she was too young and single for a lot of the cruises and increased the amount of hiking trips with the girls. The past several years, she had been discovering countries and cultures one step at a time.

She put the town of River Bend, Wisconsin, on the map when she set her first novel here. She was married once, for a brief time. Duncan had died in a car crash less than a year after they were married. She remained here in River Bend where she and my mom were raised. My mom had attended Jameson College, where she met my dad. After they were married, they moved to St. Paul, Minnesota, with me in tow, and my brother came along a few years later.

Shortly after my arrival here two years ago, I was told that EG was actually my birth mom, and because of extraordinary circumstances, my mom and dad had lovingly taken me as their own. It will be forever that I see them as Mom and Dad and EG as my aunt.

Sixteen minutes and two-and-a-half miles after leaving the liquor store, I walked in the kitchen. The drive was only three minutes; the rest was looking for parking and walking to the house.

EG met me with a strange look. "I suggested beer with the pizza for the two of us, right? A case seems a bit of an overkill."

"I got a six-pack of the Italian beer you like for you and Sherrie. By the way, you are the only person who goes to Italy and comes back with a favorite new beer and not a new favorite wine. I got some IPA for Pete. I believe there is still some light beer in the fridge for me. The empty box is for Sherrie."

"Why don't you change out of your suit and get comfy while I get the pizza," EG said.

"I could've picked it up while I was out. Let me go. Still have my keys in my hand and the car is relatively close," I offered.

"Nope. The delivery wait time is too long for Ted's, so I'm gonna get it. You will have time to change and contemplate that box I have for you."

I took four steps farther into the kitchen and looked over to the dining room table to see a six-inch box wrapped in sparkling baby-blue paper with a white bow.

EG picked up her car keys and was almost out the door when she said, "I'm not losing my mind. I know it's not your birthday, Christmas, or some other holiday. It is something I have been wanting to give you. Do not open it until I return as it takes some explaining. You are more than welcomed to pick it up and shake, but fair warning, that wrapping paper has more glitter than the floor of a strip club at two a.m. About a pound of it will stick to you even if you pick it up by the bow. I will be back in ten."

She was out the door before I could get out one question.

CHAPTER THREE

STILL AT THE HOUSE.

EG was just out of sight when I finished texting Sherrie:

> What do you know about the box?
> Don't play like you don't know.
> Is there anything I should know?

I spent the next eight minutes toggling between annoyed at Sherrie's non-reply and deciding if the outfit of choice should be comfy sweats or slightly glammed up if we were to go out after the unveiling. The closet was full of choices since Pete and I were headed to Durham, North Carolina, on Thursday for the weekend. I'd been keeping up with laundry so I could pack tonight.

A black long-sleeve, dropped-shoulder cotton top with jeans was the perfect compromise. A quick stop in the bathroom to check my makeup in case this was a photo op moment. I couldn't imagine sad news being gift wrapped.

Three minutes later, I was downstairs. Curiosity got the best of me, and I lifted the box by the bow. It seemed the only weight came from the wrapping paper. I looked around the living room for a camera to see if this was a test about touching the box or not and then laughed at myself. EG was not the type to screw with a person. If she said there was something in the box and that I should get comfy, then that was what it was and it was no game.

For the next two minutes, I was so giddy with anticipation I got paper plates and napkins from the kitchen twice. The seventy-five-year-old house had a modern large square kitchen with an island and now paper plates and napkins on it, as did the dining room table that sat between the kitchen and living room. The '80s song "What a Feeling" by Irene Cara was reeling loudly in my head that I hadn't turned on the TV or music or even heard EG come in the front door through the porch.

"You couldn't resist, could you?" EG asked. "You got glitter across your hips, you must've wiped your hands across your jeans."

"Busted. So, is now the time?"

"Step away from the box," EG instructed. "You need food in you first."

I stuck out my tongue like a bratty preschooler. "Fine, only because it's pizza, and well, because you're in charge."

I grabbed two beers from the fridge, handed EG one as she pointed for me to sit at the head of table, and she took the seat next to me. She flipped open the pizza box. We each took a slice and clinked our beer bottles together, echoing, "Cheers."

"This is exciting. It's always fun giving someone something cool. I want you to know once you open the box, it is yours and there are no 'take-backs' from me and definitely no 'I can't accept this' nonsense from you."

"Now you have me nervous." I dropped the slice and grabbed a napkin to wipe my hand and chin. EG, meanwhile, perfectly navigated beer, pizza, conversation, and rattling my brain.

"Maybe you should have a second slice before you open it up. Keep the ratio of pizza over that of the beer."

Butterflies danced in my belly so I rapidly fed them two slices of pizza and listened to EG.

"It is so amazing the life you built here in River Bend. Two years ago, you came here to help me get through chemo and basically made yourself home here."

"To be fair, it's your home and I just settled into a comfy corner, thanks to you," I said and took the last swing of the beer, surprising myself with how fast I'd consumed twelve ounces while nervously excited.

"I may have given you a room, but you got yourself a career, a great guy, friends in the community, and you brought in one of your best friends, Sherrie, to share it with."

I corrected EG again, "You brought Sherrie here, and I just rapidly agreed."

"Potato pa-ta-toe. Let's agree you are set here, at least for a while."

"Absolutely. Pete has to his finish graduate program. We may or may not—"

"But you are staying for a while?" EG interjected.

I nodded and took the shiny box EG held out to me.

"I think that is great. While you are putting roots down, temporary or otherwise, I've hardly been here and I have a complete life in Chicago. The relationship you and I have means more to me than anything in the world. Especially when the whole truth came out about me being your birth mom and Katie Lyn and Matthew raising you as their own and you still accepting me as your aunt."

12

"It was an extraordinarily thing for you to do. Watching your sister raise me and keeping your secret. We are family no matter the titles. Although 'World's Best Aunt' is a pretty good title for you."

We locked eyes. EG smiled. I saw her start to tear up.

Just above a whisper, she said, "Open it now."

I pulled the bow off, tore the tape at the bottom, and let the wrapped paper fall to the floor. Unfortunately, some of the glitter stayed on my hands. I lifted the lid of the plain white box, and there was a key sitting on white tissue paper.

EG explained, "It's the key to the house."

"Oh, I have a key. Somewhere. Not sure the last time we locked the door." Confusion swept over me. Nerves were gone, and the butterflies left. I held the key and looked at EG who was now smiling with full tears running down her cheeks, and a dull buzz started deep in my head.

"As you know, I have spent such little time here over the last several years. I'm either home in Chicago or traveling. I love my time with you girls, but my life isn't here anymore. My writing can be done anywhere."

"We will take good care of the house for you," I said.

"No. You won't," EG replied.

My hands started sweating, stomach flipping into the bottom of a pit, and I dropped my arm holding the key. "You told Sherrie already. You are selling, and we gotta move. That's why she's collecting the boxes."

EG's burst of laughter did nothing to break my slump. She leaned over and put her hands on my knees. "Darling, no. You will not take good care of the house for me. You will take good care of your house. I am giving you the house."

EG leaned back and waited for me to say something. I know I got a lot wrong in the last two minutes, but if she thought I could form some words, boy, was she ever wrong.

After a minute, she finally said, "Yes, I am giving you the house. The papers and deed should be here tomorrow or the next day. I thought wrapping up the key was more cool than some legal mumbo-jumbo stuff."

"Okay." I formed a whole word and felt good about that as I was still processing what she was saying.

"The only condition I have for this is . . ."

"Of course, anything," I said.

"Understand this is your house. You do with it as you wish. Don't keep it as a shrine or stuck in this time period. Make it yours! Paint, wallpaper, convert your room to a yoga studio, finally finish the basement and make another guest room for me or when your parents visit. There is no mortgage, but you will have property taxes and all of that, but I think you can handle it. My lawyer, Bill Ryan, can go over everything with you or get your own."

"Ah, ok." I couldn't feel my body.

EG was smiling and staring, and it was finally hitting me. "You are serious."

"Absolutely. Please spare me and you the 'I can't accept this' speech. I would hate to undo all the legal paperwork. So, for the sake of saving my lawyer some work of reversing everything, just go with it. Your parents know and are cool with it.

"Holy shit!" I stood up, and EG greeted my outstretched arms and we hugged. "Thank you! Thank you! Thank you! Although it does not seem like enough just to say thank you."

"That's all I need," EG said and gave me one last squeeze before she let me go. She grabbed her beer bottle. "Cheers and congrats."

"Wait, I need another beer, you?"

"I still have half my first beer. Plus, I am leaving in an hour for Chicago. Tomorrow I have a couple of appointments and things I need to line up before my trip."

"England, right?"

"I'm meeting the girls there before we hike around Guernsey Island, then over to Paris."

"That sounds amazing, minus that hiking."

"You know, that sounds weird coming from a runner like you. At least I get to see the sights, but you fly past everything."

"Not at my slow speed. And I avoid wicked hills that you gravitate towards." I grabbed a second beer, popped the top, and took a long drink. My cheeks were flushed and my upper body was sweating like crazy, so I stood in the open door of the refrigerator for a minute.

When I finally sat back down, grasping the beer like an appendage in my right hand and, in my left, held the key by the edges like a microscope slide. Looking at it and analyzing to understand what this means and was it real?

EG stood up and patted my shoulder. "You know that key has no magical powers. To be honest, I had mixed feelings about this."

"Absolutely, this is too much." I moved the key toward her, but she brushed my hand back and laughed again.

"Get it in your head that this is yours. My second thoughts on this were only for the concern about the shape of the house. Was I giving you a lemon and a burden."

"How can you say that? This house is amazing," I said.

"As a home, it is amazing. Strip away all the emotion, and what do you have in this house? An unfinished basement with an old propane heating tank that needs proper removal, an unattached garage in a town with brutal winters, a bathroom upstairs that needs updating, thick built-in bookcases from twenty years ago, a kitchen designed to someone else's taste, and it's all here in small town River Bend. Sell it and run. I am good with that too."

"I think am more dumbfounded now than when I opened the box. It was an incredible gift, no matter what you're saying."

"Unfortunately, maybe we are both right. The house is a gift and a burden," EG said.

Those words would haunt me for the rest of my life.

CHAPTER FOUR

A day or days later . . . . after the other incident. Well, there had been several incidents this was just another one. The big one that put Pete in the hospital.

Kay and Jenna came over and brought Sherrie and me dinner from Towne's Diner. We sat around the kitchen island, and Jenna left for two minutes to retrieve the soup she had mistakenly dropped off at Jorge's and gave him his extra blue cheese for his wings.

"Jorge, doesn't want to join us?" Sherrie asked.

"He is finishing cutting the last of the wood baseboards and wants to get it done tonight."

"Thanks for dinner. What do we owe you?" I said.

"It's on us." Kay and Jenna exchanged a look, and Kay continued, "There are also some blueberry scones from Peach's for the morning or whenever."

I had finally managed to get more than one piece of lettuce on my fork, and Sherrie finally got that bag a of soup crackers she had struggled with for two minutes opened when we put them down and in unison asked, "What's up?"

Jenna answered first, "Ah, so, um, we figured we had to tell you. Was it the scones that gave it away?"

"Peach's closed a couple of hours ago. So this has to be something big if you waited to get dinner before coming here," Sherrie said.

"Keep eating," Jenna said.

Sherrie rapidly took a couple of spoonfuls of soup.

"If you put down the spoon and just drink the soup, it will be faster," I said.

"I am chilled and just need something warm before I have my sandwich," Sherrie said.

Jenna laid it out for us, "So the town is beginning to take sides. The word about the lawsuit got out and people have very strong opinions. It was high top of conversation in the break room."

"It's a feeding frenzy up on the hill," Kay said. She worked as activity chair and receptionist at the fifty-five plus community, Chambray Community. "The old folks love gossip and now to analyze and be able pick sides; this is like a kid at Halloween."

My hand went to touch the scab on my forehead, and a crusty piece of skin fell into my salad.

Sherrie pulled my plate away and dumped it in the trash, "That was gross. Take half my sandwich and stop touching your head." I reached for the bag with the scones, but she pushed it out of reach and said, "Have some real food first."

Kay continued, "The ladies at lunch changed up their seats. Do you know how big that is. There is a such a hierarchy and clique at the senior living center, and this is breaking all the circles. The old folks are worse than high school girls."

"Just be prepare for the whispers and stares when you are out," Jenna said.

"It's weird how it is split. Not all the old white dudes are for Phil, but he is respected in the community and Patty, his wife, is related to half the town. People like Pete, but not everyone knows him. Pete's parents are well liked. His father was plant manager for decades. The Morris family name is really solid. You are young and new, but EG is gold in this town. However, her being absent so much doesn't do much in favor of you. No one knows she moved away permanently. That is one side. The other side says there is too much evidence about fault."

"They figure you guys are after money and revenge," Jenna said.

"There is no money to be had. If we pursue, it would only be countersuing for lawyer fees and to basically shut him up. Not even going after hospital bills."

"This could be big money for you and Pete," replied Jenna.

"We're not interested."

"I could use big money," Kay said to no one in particular.

"I could use a trip to Rome," Sherrie added softly.

"We don't even know if they are suing. Probably waiting for a full police report which will prove Pete did nothing wrong. Something just happened in the store when he was there."

Jenna spoke again, "People are following the money, the rumors and possible arrests."

Sherrie sat upright. "Maybe that guy is trying to serve you court papers. Police can't find Pete criminally negligible but maybe a civil suit."

I exchanged looks with Jenna and Kay and then all three of us stared at Sherrie.

"Maddie came by the rental office today. She asked how you are doing and then said two of the regular guests had inquired how you were doing. No, I don't know who, so you will have to ask Maddie. Then she said some other guy asked if you were back to work yet. She had not seen him before, and he just left without saying anything else. Maddie laughed when she said she barely remembers the guy being there. Almost like she imagined the exchange. You may need to go back to work soon if she is overworked and imagining things."

I said nothing so Sherrie added, "The last part was a joke. Just trying to lighten the mood."

CHAPTER FIVE

SUNDAY AFTER THAT TUESDAY.

Pete and I parked two blocks from EG's, I mean, my house, and we walked holding hands and pulling our luggage. Several months earlier, a pipe had broken below the street. Ever since then, the road has been dug up and with no end in sight. One broken water pipe led to a second break, and the weather has not been helpful. Frozen temperatures and record rainfall had delayed the project to where the city has even stopped giving an estimated completion date.

"We could have stayed at your place tonight and not trudge through this mess," I said.

Pete was slow to answer. "You have a better washing machine here, and the dryer doesn't take ninety minutes."

"We are doing laundry tonight?" I stopped walking, dropped his hand and spun the newly acquired engagement right on my left hand. "Honeymoon is over before it started."

Pete pulled me close to him, linking our arms as he held my elbows to raise me up just enough for him whisper in my ear, "It's just beginning. Love you! Now let's go, I know you're excited to share this with Sherrie, and I kinda wanna watch you tell her." He spun the ring on my finger and pinched my elbow to get me moving. Girls always want to show off their ring, but I wanted to show off Pete. The ring too was beautiful and unique. I couldn't believe he remembered and had one made including the one comment I made about the original one we had seen.

He grabbed my suitcase and starting walking ahead. I looked at the house and could hear Sherrie's music from the windows. Muted light was coming through the sheets we had hung up on the front porch. Despite the rainy March weather, the road construction was sending endless plumes of dirt, dust, and everything else into the air and into the house.

Sherrie and I had paid seven dollars and twenty-six cents for bedsheets at Goodwill and then nailed them up. We enclosed the screen porch and were able to keep the airflow going when the dust settled after a storm. Two of them started off as baby bird eggshell blue and now looked like the khaki shorts worn by the Southwest flight attendants.

I held open the screen door for Pete, but he insisted I go first. He dropped our bags on the porch with such force I thought he cracked a floorboard. "Are you sure we're good coming here?"

He spun me around to the front door, push it opened, and gently pushed me through the threshold to the sound of a champagne bottle popping open, cheers and shouts of congratulations.

It was a blur of images and shock. Pete stepped in behind me and wrapped his arms around me and said into my ear, "I was only informed to come to the house twelve minutes ago with a text. I was to make sure we came here."

"You hate secrets."

"There is a difference between surprises and secrets." Pete may have said more, but I couldn't hear anything over the crowd screaming and the paper horns leftover from New Year's Eve.

I was pulled into a hug from my dad who was signing "Maneater" by Hall and Oats.

"Can't you pick a better song?" I pleaded.

"Any other song will make me cry, and I don't want to lose my man card in front of my new soon-to-be son-in-law."

Seconds later, he was pulled away from me by mom. My dad skipped the half handshake/half slap on the back and gave Pete a full-on hug. My parents and younger brother, Connor, were the only people I had called after Pete proposed. I wanted to tell Sherrie in person.

"Honey, I am so happy for you," My mom said.

"Did you do all of this? Drove all the way and got everyone here and set this up?"

"All we did was drive here. This was Sherrie and Mia's doing. I did let out your secret but only because Sherrie kept asking for updates anytime you two went on a trip and thought it might happen. How could I keep the celebration from happening?"

Pete's mom, Peggy, and his dad, Don, were the next to congratulate us. Sherrie and Mia were up next. Mia, Sherrie, and I and a few others had shared an apartment during college. Sherrie and Mia had been jumping up and down waiting their turn, spilling more champagne than they were consuming.

"You guys planned this? How did you know? Mia, when did you get to town? Do you have to leave tonight so you can work tomorrow?

How many people are here? This is nuts! You did this for us?"

"Just stop talking and show us the big o' rock," Mia said.

"It ain't no rock, but a braid of ruby and emerald stones on a ring of black gold. Isn't it amazing?" I squealed and held up my hand.

"Holy shit! That is incredible." Sherrie was nearly breathless. "He did gooood! Give us the details. Your mom wouldn't tell us anything expect it was go-time for the party."

"Why did you think it was going to happen this weekend? I was surprised."

Sherrie answered, "Of course you were. I pretty much thought it after your first month of dating that is was logical you two be together forever. However, it was a couple of months ago I had come up the stairs, you were in the shower and I saw Pete standing at your dresser slipping rings on his finger. I thought he was trying to get your ring size."

"That was my idea." CiCi, one of Pete's roommates, came up and gave me a hug.

"You knew he was going to do this?"

"Not directly. Like Sherrie said, it was obvious watching you together. I just started dropping random comments. Like, 'I can't believe my cousin thought his fiancée has such fat fingers. Now I'm going to have to listen to them complain about her losing the ring. All he had to do was try on some of her rings. He spent too much money. He should have gone to that place east of the Twin Cities.' By the way, I have no cousin that is currently engaged."

"That was smart and thank you. It fits perfectly."

"That is special. How are you going to pair that with the wedding band? Are you getting the big stone on the wedding day?" Mallory asked while she shifted eighteen-month-old Liam to her right hip. For Sherrie and me over the last year and half, Mallory had gone from most disliked resident of River Bend to pseudo-friend to kinda likable friend. She and I had a common ex-boyfriend.

"No rock for me. We haven't talked too much about it as this only happened about seventy-two hours ago. We thought maybe just a slender band to match Pete's."

"I don't buy it. Every girl wants the sparkle." That was from Marcus, Pete's brother.

"Not this one," Pete said and gave me a nudge. "See, I listen."

"This is so unusual. How did you know she would like something like that?" Mallory asked.

"When we were in Pasadena for the Rose Bowl game, she dragged me through some antique shop and was transfixed by a similar ring," Pete said. His face was red with embarrassment when he realized over half the room was listening to him. He also had a huge grin on his face because he knew he'd nailed it with the custom ring.

I added, "That gentleman said that was the only thing in the store not for sale. I asked why he displayed at the counter for everyone to see. He said it had belonged to his late wife, and this way he gets to see a part of her everyday."

CiCi said, "So you got the ring right, but what about a vacation you both want to do. Hope the honeymoon will be better than your last two trips. It was a football game in Pasadena, and before that it was baseball game in Boston and now basketball in Durham. How about a beach vacation or like when Pete took off for nine months and traveled through Europe, but stay in something better than a youth hostel."

I looked at Pete, and he squeezed my hand and smiled at me.

I turned to the group and said, "Thanks for thinking of me, but these trips are for both of us. On one of our first dates while waiting for the movie to start, we wandered into the used bookstore. Pete found this coffee table book titled *The Sports Bucket List, 101 Sights Everyone Must See*. We made a pact to see every event. Trust me, I will turn the Daytona 500 race into a few days at the beach, and there are some international events. Monaco Grand Prix is high on my list."

"Before we hear about their future travels, I would like to wish Claudia and Pete . . ." My dad stuttered his words. The man was never shy. He could hold his own in a room of any size.

Tears instantly flowed from me when I looked at him.

The man usually has nerves of steel, but he has a bigger heart. Before he lost it completely, he had to keep it short, "Claudia's mother and I couldn't be happier for the two of them. We never doubted she would find a guy. We are just excited it's Pete. Lets give them a cheer."

Everyone gave a shout of joy. I heard cheers from the kitchen from people I didn't even know were in the house. After the round of cheers ended, my father collected a round of boos by nearly everyone in the house when he said, "Now who is up for karaoke?"

In some ways, I wished the karaoke machine would have shown up at EG's, I mean, my house. The next morning, the house probably wouldn't be full of six-plus hungover people and the start of something I could never imagine.

CHAPTER SIX

Back on the porch weeks after the first incident
days after the second incident.

Someone had put a small rubber ball in my hand. Slouched down deep into the sofa, I bounced the ball off the support beam across from me mindlessly. The rhythmic motion kept me from being completely sewn into the couch.

CiCi walked up the steps to the screened-in porch and didn't bother knocking. She put down a box next to the door, waited for ball to drop back in my hand, walked around the table I had my feet on, and sat in the comfy chair to my right. "Something is not right," she said.

There was no need to respond. It was obvious something wasn't right. Pete was dead and not everything being said about him was good.

She continued. "I went to see his parents to talk about the rent. I had gone to the leasing office for the house. Just to figure out our options since we have six months left on the lease, and without Pete's share, I thought Sam may have a hard time with rent."

Bounce

"Before I could get to the real point, Pete's brother, Marcus, started yelling that it's no time to be discussing this. He threw me out of the house before his mother even said a word."

Bounce

"I will cover whatever Pete owes. Just text me, actually, I don't know where my phone is so you should probably go inside and write it down," I said.

"Its just that . . ."

"CiCi, you better not be there. I saw your car around the block." Marcus's voice was getting louder as he walked up the sidewalk towards the house.

"Oh, crap. I didn't mean . . . sorry. Didn't think he would follow me. I am just going to go out the back." One second she was in the chair, and the next, she was in the house.

Bounce

Marcus knocked on the screen door, calling out for CiCi. I ignored him. He pressed his face to the screen and eventually let himself in. "Hey, Claudia. I'm looking for CiCi. Is she here bugging you about money?"

Bounce

Bounce

Bounce

He didn't wait for me to answer. "I can't stand it these days. All these people and their pity for our loss. At least they are trying. CiCi didn't even bother with any of that. Just coming after his money." Marcus paced in the far corner, nearly tripping over Sherrie's bike.

Bounce

Bounce

Marcus kept talking, "You are not going to say anything. Too stunned like I am. How like Pete to be sharing a house with someone like that. I can't believe it . . ."

Bounce

Sherrie's mother, Evie Lawrence, opened the screen door carrying three white bags. "Marcus, I could hear you down the street. You wouldn't be bothering Claudia here are you?"

"It's just that CiCi has been to my mother's and . . ."

"Sherrie, come take the food," Evie said and only had to wait three seconds for Sherrie to pop onto the porch and take all the bags, allowing Evie the ability to put her hand on Marcus's shoulder, steering him towards the screen door. "I don't see CiCi here, and from the sound of your voice, if she were here, she would know not to come out here. If we see her, we will pass on your message."

Marcus was out the door and down the steps before he knew it. Thankfully, he went quietly away.

Bounce

"You ok, Claudia." It was not so much of a question from Evie but a survey of the porch. She went inside and left me with my ball.

Sherrie and CiCi joined me on the porch twenty-seven bounces later, Sherrie carrying a tray of Chinese food and CiCi three beers.

CiCi sat next to me on the couch and handed me an egg roll while Sherrie confiscated my ball midair. She took the seat in the chair that CiCi had vacated when Marcus showed up.

The egg roll got one bite before I tossed it on the table, and the beer, well, that I consumed when I started pacing. I didn't know it then, but good friends and Chinese food can do a lot for a person only if you take advantage when the shit hits the fan.

CHAPTER SEVEN

The Monday morning after the Surprise Engagement Party.

Pete and I woke up at seven Monday morning spooning on top of my bed covers. I think we had collapsed on the bed at two a.m. and hadn't moved all night. We were still wearing our same clothes as the day before.

I spun the ring on my finger and smiled. Pete remembering my affection for the antique ring we had seen a few months ago made this so special.

Pete asked, "Are you trying to screw it off your finger?"

"Not in a million years. You ask that again, and you will be in trouble," I said.

Pete took a shower and threw on clean clothes from his suitcase. He looked amazing and not like he had partied for ten hours last night. He went downstairs for breakfast while I showered. I pulled my wet hair into a ponytail and spent sixty seconds doing my makeup. That lack of effort showed in my appearance.

I walked downstairs, pausing as I surveyed the amount of red plastic cups around the room. It wasn't so bad, and at least there weren't empty pizza boxes everywhere. There was an unidentified pair of feet sticking out from a blanket on the couch. EG's bedroom door was shut, and I didn't have time to check who was on the porch couch because the smell of coffee was drawing me to the kitchen.

I stopped short at the bookcase. Something caught me eye. My hand trembled and a tear fell from my eye.

"She crying again. Pete, you are now on deck permanently to handle Claudia," Mia said from the kitchen.

"I thought you were sleeping in EG's room," I said.

"It's actually your room now. Remember this is not her house anymore. I took the pullout sofa in Sherrie's room. What's got you so worked up this morning already?"

Sherrie wandered over. "Oh, man! That is the best engagement gift ever. I thought throwing the surprise party rocked."

"I don't get it," Mia said.

"It's a message from Ellie." Next to a picture of Pete and me was a treasured plastic toy green army man piece. Last year, Sherrie and I had befriended then eighteen-year-old Ellie and her eight-year-old brother, Ben. They had a tough living situation and would sometimes have to stay at other people's houses. Ellie had told us she always left a green army man around for Ben to know he was safe. Either in his backpack, sleeping bag, or jacket pocket. After we helped them out, she secretly left Sherrie and me each a green army man by a picture of the two of us. Now I was looking at a rare piece of two army men that didn't get separated during manufacturing sitting in front of the picture of Pete and me.

Sherrie and I had become self-proclaimed super aunts to Ben. Last year, when Mallory was single, pregnant, and about to move into a home she could barely afford, I suggested Ellie and Ben move in with her. It had been incredible to watch this unlikely duo of Mallory and Ellie create a beautiful home for the boys.

"I didn't even see her," I said.

"Ben was here," Pete said when we all walked back into the kitchen. "That should be our cake topper."

"Nice idea, but it's a little small," I said.

"I don't think Ellie even stayed until you guys finally got here. Too many people for her liking. She doesn't do crowds. Ben went home with Mallory," Sherrie said.

"That guy was staring at her like she was going to nick something," Mia said.

"What guy?" Sherrie asked.

"Tall, grayish hair of what is left of it, late sixties, maybe early seventies."

"Phil, owner of the hardware store," Sherrie answered.

"How did he end up at the party? I know it's River Bend and all but, really?" I asked.

"You're right about it being River Bend. Saturday, when I was buying the booze, he was in the liquor store and helped me carry out some bottles. It was natural to invite him. Dale, the owner of the liquor store, was going to swing by too, but he must have gotten stuck at his granddaughter's confirmation party," Sherrie said.

Pete said, "I used to think he was a nice guy, but he got all weird when I told him I could handle the wall. I tried politely telling him I got it. He was talking to me like I was five years old and had picked up my dad's buzz saw. He also assumed I punched the wall. I stopped short of F off only because my future in-laws were two feet away." Pete blushed when he said future in-laws. He melted my heart again, he was so happy.

"The wall?" Mia asked.

I tilted my head towards the living room and to the picture frame around a hole in the wall. "Last week, the night EG gave me the house on her way out, she took a hammer and pounded into the drywall and said, 'Now you have to fix this place up and make it your own.' "

"I meant to ask about that. Who put the frame around it? Actually, don't answer that, it could be any one of the three of you and you probably had some ceremony around it. God, I miss living with you guys. I think I could even like living with Pete." Mia laughed. "Anyone know why my feet are black?"

Sherrie was quick to answer and mockingly so with the use of air quotes. "You decided while everyone was dancing in the backyard, it would be better or in your own words, 'more authentic' if you were barefoot."

"Did I really use the word *authentic*? Please don't answer that either. I better get going if I am going to make it to work before the afternoon meeting."

"I was hoping you could stay longer," I said.

"The past few months, I have been tentatively scheduled to be off each Monday morning. Ever since Sherrie put into operation PACE-P, 'Pete and Claud's Engagement Party.' By the way, everyone in my office says congratulations, but I have to get back."

Hugs were exchanged all around. Mia declared, "Wedding dress shopping by me in Madison or Twin Cities near your mom. I am not coming back until your street is fixed. You guys have been talking about it for two months; I don't see what you guys love about this town. Can't seem to get one street done in a timely manner. This house I get, but not so much the town."

It was the town that saved me and the house.

CHAPTER EIGHT

After waving goodbye to Mia, my brother came in from the porch. He stood in front of the open fridge. "Are you out of Coke?"

"In the cooler on the floor over there," Sherrie said. "Don't tell me that's your breakfast?"

"No way, man. Mom brought all this food yesterday."

"I totally forgot she put stuff in the basement. Help me carry it up, Connor. Claud, grab the stuff from the fridge." They returned two minutes later carrying coffee cake, mom's homemade muffins, and some juice.

My mother had fresh fruit and an egg casserole and of course our favorite potato cornflake casserole waiting for us in fridge. Sherrie, Pete, Connor, and I all started to dig in.

Conner threw a spoon across the room, over the dinning table into the living room to the person under the blanket on the couch. "Get up, or I won't make my eleven o'clock class."

We heard some mumbling and watched a body roll over. Conner picked up another spoon, but Sherrie grabbed it and handed him two silicone hot pads. "Two more throws and then you need to go over there. You are not chucking metal across the room and breaking one of her living room windows."

I laughed. "I can't believe this house is mine. It's crazy."

"More crazy than Pete putting that on your finger," Connor said.

"In some ways, yes. The house was unexpected. Ring or no ring, I just always figured us to be with each other."

"That is so sweet I almost want to throw up," Sherrie snipped. "Just kidding. That is a beautiful way to put it."

We watched Connor throw the hot pads to no success in rousting the guy on the couch I'd guessed to be his college dorm mate, Simon. They had a ninety-minute ride back to campus and that didn't include having to look for parking.

I had a sudden thought. "Con, are you good with me and the house? It's a big gift."

"You think I want a piece of this? No, thanks. River Bend is not for me."

"It's just everything has always been even with us," I said.

"Haven't really thought about it." A smile slid across his face. "Maybe I will get EG's condo in Chicago. Although she is too young for me get in the will anytime soon, and I don't think she has a another home somewhere else yet. Maybe I do want a piece of this."

"Willing to split property taxes?"

"On second thought, it's all yours. And from what Pete said last night, with the renovations you are thinking about, I got no cash. Enjoy your house."

"We will," I said and held up my coffee mug to Pete and Sherrie. She was a bit late with cheers.

Conner scooped up a mouthful of the egg dish and said, "Speaking of cash, your brother, Marcus, had a lot to say about a prenup. He was pumping me for information about our family and finances. He wouldn't drop the subject. If it wasn't for someone dancing into me and pushing me to ground, I probably would have gone after him."

"Sorry, he's a bit fixated on stupid stuff. Thank you for not knocking him out. Save it for me," Pete said.

"Really?" Sherrie asked. "I thought all you Morris kids were close."

"As brothers, we have the duty to protect our siblings at all costs, yet we are also the ones who get to throw the first punch. It works both ways. Since I don't think anyone as decked him since Anna Croskic in second grade when he took her spot in the recess line, I get to toss the first punch."

"What I do want is the name of that place you stayed for spring break. What's that guy's name, your roommate from college, Trager. I thinks he's from here too. He was telling us about the place in Florida six of you stayed at dirt cheap. That sounded like a sweet trip," Connor said.

"I'm not even sure that place is still there. It's been six years, and it should have be condemned back then. I will see what I can come up with for you," Pete answered.

"I'd skip the Florida beach trip and repeat Pete's European backpacking trip. But only once my head stops hurting, I have money, and no school or work schedule. I could use a few days in Paris," Sherrie shared with us and then asked, "Connor, is that Simon, your roommate on the couch? And when did Maddie leave? Kay? Jenna? Trager? CiCi?" She pushed her plate of food away and put her elbows on the island to hold her head up.

"When did anyone leave? I remember my parents leaving around nine since my dad had an early meeting this morning and they had a two-hour drive. Pete's parents left before that. I don't know too much after the all the parents left since I think that was when someone decided we need to do a shot every time some said the words *wedding, ring* or *congratulations*. I thought we were done buying apple schnapps."

Sherrie downed a mug of coffee before she answered. "The game was Connor's idea and Jorge brought the schnapps. He made point of saying it was not so much a gift as it was someone left it at his house, and he was just passing it on."

"I still can hear music ringing in my ears. Do I need to make more coffee?" I asked and received a chorus of *yes*. "Do we need to wake Jenna? It's nearly eight?"

"Where is she?" Sherrie asked.

"I was assuming in EG's room. That's her purse on the counter behind you," I said.

Just then, we heard the first-floor bedroom door open, but to our surprise, Maddie shuffled into the kitchen. Maddie was a River Bend native attending Jameson College and my favorite coworker. And like my twenty-year-old brother, liked to party on free beer especially when they didn't have to drive anywhere and no one was asking for your ID.

Pete stood up and gave her a spot to sit. She mumbled good morning and declined juice and coffee. She put her hands on her face and then rubbed the sand out of her eyes before lifting her head. "Do you have Coke and maybe an aspirin or two?"

I grabbed the aspirin bottle from the junk drawer and gave Connor a look and a head nod. It was when he handed the soda over without looking at her I realized something must have gone on with them last night. Not wanting to embarrass Maddie, I would have to wait on calling out my brother.

"Oh, god. You people are awake already." Jenna walked the back door carrying her shoes. "I need my purse and keys. I am gonna be so late."

"If you want, you can shower here and borrow whatever clothes you might need," I said.

"Thanks, I just might do that." Jenna grabbed her purse and walked silently around us, sitting at the island.

"The upstairs bathroom is open; towels are in the closet," I said.

"Got it," Jenna said and walked into the living room.

Sherrie followed up with, "Just one more thing."

Jenna slowly turned around and waited for more instructions, but Sherrie asked what we were all thinking. "Walk of shame or stride of pride?"

Jenna turned back, kept walking and replied, "It's never shame."

Sherrie and I gave her a round of applause, and I whispered, "Who could it have been?"

Pete rolled his eyes, and Sherrie and I went through the list of everyone at party when we heard Jorge's motorcycle pull out of his driveway next door. He was the only person on the block not affected by the on-going street repair as he just rode his motorcycle around the barricades.

"He must have drank a lot last night. He is usually at his shop by seven," I said.

"OMG! Jenna was carrying her shoes. She walked from next door," Sherrie said and together we said, "Jorge!"

Sherrie sat upright like a frozen statue. This could only have meant one thing, and with her hangover, she was getting nowhere with the mental math.

I said, "Seven-or eight-year difference. She is a mature twenty-eight-year-old and he is a cool thirty-fiveish.

"I think it works," Sherrie said.

"Agreed," I replied.

Sherrie headed upstairs to help Jenna find some clothes to borrow.

Pete rolled his eyes again and took our plates to the dishwasher. Connor and Maddie kept their heads down, confirming for me something had happened with them last night.

My mom texted me to make sure Connor and Simon were on the road. She followed up with some links to wedding dress stores near her.

Connor and I spent two minutes negotiating how much of my mother's baked goods he could take. I should have known he was up to something when he settled for only four of my mother's muffins. Five minutes later when he and Simon walked out the door, he thanked me for Ms. Clara's peach pie he was sneaking out.

Ms. Clara's pies were a highly sought-after commodity in River Bend. She used to own Peach's Cafe before retiring and moving in with her sister in St. Paul. She baked anywhere from ten to twenty pies a week. Not bad for an arthritic lady in her late eighties. Most of those pies made their way to Peach's Cafe, which one of her daughters now ran. My parents lived close and got 'em straight from the oven.

One minute after Connor left, Maddie made her way out of the kitchen. She came and gave me a hug and said another congratulations on the engagement.

I wouldn't release her from the hug and said, "I have to ask you . . ."

She laughed, "Busted. Was it obvious? I couldn't even look at your brother this morning.

And don't you dare talk to him about it or bring it up at work."

"I won't say anything."

"He did sleep on the porch. I don't know why I'm explaining this you," Maddie said.

"As his sister, I don't want all the details."

"I'm trying to be cool about it, but I hope your brother texts. Not a great morning impression I'm putting off with my bedhead and morning breath."

"He still had pillow creases across his forehead, so I think you're good. I will see you at work."

Sherrie shouted from the stairs, "Maddie, when I'm at work this afternoon, I will text you some information about upcoming rentals."

Jenna trotted past Sherrie as she headed back upstairs. Jenna was wearing Sherrie's navy blouse, my black pencil skirt, and her ankle boots from yesterday.

"You clean up good and fast," I said.

"Thanks for the skirt. I will get it back to you this week. Sherrie already peppered me with questions about Jorge. I don't have time to rehash it."

"I'll get the scoop from her. Grab something off the island to eat. Are you parked close? Do you need a ride?"

"Somehow I got a spot around the block. Thankfully, I forgot your street is torn up otherwise I would've walked with Kay and not had my car here. Hopefully, Judge Konrad had an eight a.m. meeting and hasn't noticed I'm gonna be twenty minutes late."

After Jenna left, I went upstairs to find Pete sorting through our luggage, and one of the most disturbing scenes in Sherrie's room.

CHAPTER NINE

Back on the Porch after Pete's incident.

"Something is not adding up right," CiCi said. "I don't mean to pry but how much did you guys lay out about your finances."

Silence. My hand kept twitching for the ball.

"Claud!" snapped Sherrie. "I will give this back to you if you promise not bounce it for ten minutes while we eat. You need to eat more. Don't make my mother come out to the porch. She will go full Evie-Lawrence-mom-power-ranger mom, and we don't need that on the porch. She is getting some work down while she eats."

"Huh?"

"That's it! Snap to it lady!" Sherrie said while she swept my feet off the coffee table.

CiCi slid over the tray of food and shoved a paper plate in my hand.

"Listen, we got some figuring out to do. CiCi has some information here, and I work better when you and I function as a team."

CiCi scooped some fried rice on my plate and put a fork in my hand. "Look, you don't have to tell, and I don't know how to ask about other people's finances. All that makes me uncomfortable. I am living month to month and don't see it getting much better if I continue with a master's of fine arts and try to support myself as an artist. I am just going to tell you what I learned."

"I said I would pay his rent. Did I say that to you or someone else?" I took a scoop of fried rice and spit some of the rice back on the plate.

"Sorry, about that. I nuked everything. It took my mom a while to find parking after she went and got the food," Sherrie said. "Have some of the sesame chicken, it's not steaming hot."

"Claudia, listen to me." CiCi wiped orange sauce off her face and continued, "I am not asking you to pay rent or for any money. I'm trying to tell you Pete's rent is paid in until the end of lease and so is mine and Sam's. You can bet Sam and I didn't pay it."

"Any idea where that money came from?" Sherrie asked.

"My first and only thought was maybe Pete's parents so I went to talk to them. There's no way I can accept it. Appreciate it, yes, but no way. I don't live off someone else, for christsake, I'm an artist and practically took an oath of poverty. They can pay for Pete's share, I mean I am not stupid. Six months rent is a lot to cover. The conversation didn't get too far. His mom honestly looked like she didn't know what I was talking about, and before his dad could say anything, Marcus started yelling at me, so I just left. Didn't even say bye, just turned and walked out while he was going on and on. I am not so good with confrontation."

"That's the second time someone had said that some has been paid and not the other way around like half this town is saying," Sherrie said.

"What are you talking about?" I asked.

Sherrie hesitated before she spoke. "The guy that was talking about things that were taken care of."

"You mean at the funeral? You can say the word *funeral*. I think I can handle the word *funeral*. It's not like I can slip further into a hole. You and my mother don't need to come out here and hold me."

"Your mom went home yesterday morning. My mom's been here since Katie Lyn left. Both your parents are coming back tomorrow night," Sherrie said. "Mia is thinking of coming up too if there is room for her."

"Seriously?" My voice was whisper level. "I need that much help?"

Sherrie didn't say anything for a long minute, and then her eyes welled up. "I do." She put down her plate of food. "We have never been through this before. We had grandparents die and others, but no one as close and much less someone . . ."

She didn't finish that sentence. Instead, she stared at the billowing sheets fluttering in the wind. "I have no idea how to help. Everyone is at loss. In addition to wanting to make sure you are ok, we all also miss him. The whole town is a mess. Your mother has been a wreck one minute, and the other she is the glue holding this house together. There been a few more cornflake casserole moments that earn Katie Lyn the title of reigning queen in this town. She was going to miss more work, but your father convinced her to go home for a few days. Your mother only agreed to leave when my mom came up."

"I am fine just sitting here."

Sherrie and CiCi exchanged a look, disagreeing with my statement and then Sherrie asked, "Five bucks if you can tell me what day of the week it is."

"Let me have my time." I was so exhausted I didn't know if I'd said that out loud.

"We all think you get to have your time, and we need time too. However, we can't let you slip away too far on your own. Physically, you are almost there. Your scabs are mostly healed, and the cut on your arm and sprained wrists are much better. Our parents are here for all of us and us for them. Thank god, your mother shut down the meal train. Some people in River Bend are very kind, but that does not mean they should be cooking. Some of that stuff people were bringing over I couldn't identify."

"Is that why you look so nice? Your mom is here and braided her hair," I said.

"Wow, first sign of being in the moment, and you take a shot. CiCi, alert the tribe she is making upward progress, at my expense no less, but I will take it." Sherrie picked up a piece of rice off her shirt and flicked it my way. "And to answer her question, yes, my mom did my hair."

I finally looked over to the box CiCi had dropped off. "What did you bring over?"

"Some odds and ends I was going to give his parents but didn't because I rushed out. There is also something I thought you might want now before it losing his scent. It was in the basement next to the laundry machine so I don't think it was washed." CiCi reached over to the box and pulled out Pete's blue Duke University sweatshirt we bought the weekend he proposed in Durham. Her hands were covered in green paint and clay and a slice of anger swept over me thinking she had better not gotten any of it on the sweatshirt.

I pulled it over my head careful not to break any of the scabs on my forehead and cheek. As I wrapped my arms around me, I could still smell him. It was the closest thing to a hug I didn't know I needed. Sherrie hadn't moved, and I could tell she was watching my every move. At the funeral and afterwards, there were so many people hugging and touching me, it fast became smothering. It was all meant for support, but it pushed me into a corner of loneliness. My solace was on this porch, but suddenly, now drowning in his sweatshirt, I felt awake for the first time in a long time.

"What you were you guys saying? Something about money?" I said and picked up my plate of sesame chicken.

Sherrie watched me take a few bites before she said, "Mr. Alan. I think was his name. He runs the boat slips at the marina and dry dock storage. He cornered Pete's dad. Telling him the slip is paid for the summer season but wasn't sure if he should pull the boat out. He has a waitlist for people wanting the slip. Mr. Alan was emphasizing it wasn't about the fees since everything is paid. He wants everyone to enjoy the water."

CiCi jumped in, "Was he the loner guy in a suit in the back of church? Tacky to be talking money at the funeral. I'd thought maybe an uncle or something that didn't get along with the family but liked Pete. I didn't see him talking to anyone."

"He wasn't in a suit and his shirt was barely clean. I think Pete's dad was relieved to be talking about something practical. That guy just kept saying everything is now paid for, but it gets his goat when people have these beautiful boats, don't use them, and prevent others from using the slip. Pete shouldn't have been worried about it when he was sick. Spending time with family is important, but he admired how he took care of things."

"You heard the whole conversation?" CiCi asked.

"It was after the service before the luncheon in the reception hall at the restaurant. No judgment here, please, Mia and I were in the corner woofing down some sandwich rolls she nicked off the buffet table. We were starving. So we were just trying to eat quickly and not look like we were five years old eating forbidden Halloween candy. They were on the other side of the faux ficus."

CiCi's phone beeped, and she excused herself. She was late meeting up with someone at the art studio. "I will take the rest of the stuff in the box back to his parents."

"What's in it?" I asked. From the look CiCi gave Sherrie, I jumped in before Sherrie could answer, "You don't have to run everything past Sherrie or whoever else is here at the time. I am not that broken."

"It's just two of those make-your-own photo albums. Pete's sister-in-law, Rachel, put it together for him with the photos he shared with the family while on his nine-month backpacking trip through Europe. Although, he is not much of a photographer."

"Not everyone has an artist's eye like you have, CiCi. I'll take it over there," I said.

She stood up to leave, and surprisingly, I got up and gave her hug. It felt energizing and not draining. She didn't come to depressingly check on me or weigh me down with her grief. Her visit was the spark that got me thinking and therefore moving.

CHAPTER TEN

STILL THE MORNING AFTER THE ENGAGEMENT PARTY.

While Pete was in my room on his laptop looking over some material for his master's program, I went to Sherrie's room to again thank her for the awesome surprise party when I tripped over a box.

"I thought downstairs was rough and the backyard a wreck, but what is this chaos?" I scooted around two boxes and collapsed on the pullout couch Mia had slept on.

"They're moving boxes. I don't know what is not obvious about it," Sherrie said and stuffed some books into her backpack.

"I don't think there was that much old research material of EG's still here."

"Some days I think you are the smartest person I know, and other days I am not so sure. The boxes are my moving boxes."

"What, why . . . ah." My head was doing the calculations, but my heart was not equaling up what she was saying.

"Let me help you out. Several weeks ago, EG accidentally left the paperwork for the house lying out on the kitchen island. She told me she was planning giving you the house. I was so stoked for you. It was the best secret I had to keep."

"Secrets versus surprises, Pete always says. Secrets are usually bad. Surprises are good but harder to keep quiet," I said.

Sherrie raised her voice so Pete could hear her, "Pete, she is quoting you. The transformation of becoming one is already in effect. Lord, help us all!"

"Amen!" shouted Pete. "What words of wisdom is she unloading?"

"Secrets versus surprises. Good versus bad," Sherrie said.

"Words to live by," Pete shouted back.

Sherrie continued moving around the room, putting notebooks and her laptop in her backpack. The hangover must have been bad because she kept dropping the items. "With me assuming the proposal was coming soon, EG departing, and giving you the house, I assumed you two will want the house to yourself so I have been looking for a new place."

I sat up and shouted, "Pete! She's—" Before I could finish, Pete was at Sherrie's door.

"Whats up?" He asked.

"She thinks she has to move."

Pete looked at Sherrie and just simply said, "No. We cool. You just have to live through—"

Beep, beep, beep

From Sherrie's window, we heard our new morning wake-up call. A city utility truck was backing down the street. I looked at Pete, "Better go talk to him before the supervisor shows."

Pete left, and I finished his answer to Sherrie. "First, appreciate the offer to leave, but no. Pete and I talked a lot about future plans. We are starting immediately with finishing the basement and adding central air-conditioning."

"You had me at central air. It's getting easier to possibly stay."

"Is that why you got a job at the leasing office?"

"I went in one day to scope out potential rental units. No one was in the front office, and the phone kept ringing. I answered the phone twice and took messages. When Ginny, the owner, came in from the back room, I gave her the messages, and she offered me a job. I figured I would have first pick at rentals near campus coming available. The hours are part-time, and I basically get to work around my classes. Now tell me about the reno plans."

"So within the last five days, we talked a lot, and we are making some fast progress. We are making the basement into a TV area, adding a bathroom, and moving the laundry upstairs. We know that for sure, but we not sure what and when we will do the rest. Kitchen is fine, maybe not our exact taste but definitely good. Maybe get rid of those heavy bookcases in the living room, but we haven't got that far. No need for us to rush. He still has his lease, and we have to get our finances together.

"Long story short. We don't want you going anywhere anytime soon. And before you make fun of me saying 'we,' yes, Pete and I talked about you living in the house. It was kinda cute as he assumed you were going to live with us for a while, almost like a condition of me saying yes to the proposal. Don't flatter yourself either as you weren't part of the actual proposal."

Sherrie finally stopped messing with her bag and sat on the edge of her bed actually almost missing it. The hangover must have been really bad. "Speaking of the proposal, you said he got down on one knee on the sidewalk in Durham, but was there any reason he did it there? Had he been there before, and it's his favorite spot or is there some historical significance?"

My face was flushed, and I was giddy inside. I was engaged to the best guy I knew and loved. "You know that song—"

"Ohmygod, you two are made for each other. He puts up with your nonstop '80s music you're constantly humming, singing, and dancing to. What song or movie inspired this sweet thing?" She leaned over tapped my ring.

"It's that song by Marc Cohn, 'True Companion.' " I smiled and fiddled with my ring. I watched Sherrie go still like a statue. "Before you break your brain trying to figure it out, let me explain. Part of the lyrics are:

I can see us walking slowly arm in arm
Just like that couple on the corner do, 'cause
Girl I will always be in love with you."

"Still not getting the connection," she said.

"I always sang that second line as:

Just like that couple on the corner at Duke."

"Those lyrics don't make sense," Sherrie said.

"Do any lyrics make logical sense and have a definitive order? It's poetry. Anyways, Pete thought it was sweet and when he corrected me, he knew right then that was going to be the spot to propose. So, that's why he chose to go to Durham and the Duke campus so we could be the sweet old couple others strive to be."

"That is one romantic and jealous-making proposal. However you getting an '80s song lyric messed up and starting your life together on, that is bad juju."

"It's from the '90s, so we are fine."

Oh, how I wish Sherrie had been wrong.

CHAPTER ELEVEN

Back on that porch.

CiCi left, and I was now eating food from straight from each of the Chinese food cartons. Sherrie was watching me while rapid-fire texting. "As my grandma would say, what has you attacking your phone like June bugs to a light?"

She looked at me, typed again before finally responding, "Honestly?"

"When would I expect otherwise?"

"Just giving some people an update. Before you give me some strange look or ask some dumb question. Yes, there is a group chat, actually two groups, about how you are coming along. One to your parents, brother, EG, and the other with Mia, Jenna, Kay, and the occasional one to some others, but they only get a light version with pleas of don't send food. Oh, I think my mother might have a sub group that includes updates I don't know about."

I lowered the carton of fried rice I had propped near my chin and just looked at Sherrie when a tear fell from my eye. "Thank you."

"Don't you start crying and backsliding, or I have to have edit my last few texts. Current state is that you are actually eating a decent amount of food and sarcasm is back, but we will see how the rest of the night goes."

"I'm fine." My hand went up to stop whatever was going to come out of Sherrie's mouth. "I know I've said those words a thousand times, but I think I hit my bottom."

She kept quiet and waited me out, so I continued, "I'm gonna tell you something you don't need to include in your updates."

Sherrie held up hand like a Boy Scout. "Promise."

"For a minute or two or maybe thirty-eight minutes, I contemplated burning down the house. I forget all the seven stages of grief, but the anger stage was probably at its peak. I kinda hoped it would burn down parts of this town and all those who doubt Pete's integrity. I feel robbed my of sense of home. Not in this house but this community. Rumors and accusations are making me feel like an outsider. There was some biblical references of torching the town swirling in my head. Maybe not biblical but barbarian."

There was no judgment in Sherrie's voice. "What stopped you?"

"The almost newly installed central air. I thought it would be a waste of Pete's money." I forced a laugh to match Sherrie's. Couldn't let her know the thought was still there. Who would think Pete could blow up a place?

Sherrie laughed again and waited before she asked what everyone was thinking. "We never really got the point of CiCi's visit. What is the financial situation?"

CHAPTER TWELVE

Ten days after the engagement party.

"Order a beer. Just a beer," Sherrie said out of the side of her mouth when she leaned over and took her backpack off the barstool she was saving for me.

I'd met her at Draw Bar where Pete had begun working shortly after he and I had started dating. He had been working at BAR owned by my ex-boyfriend Aaron. Things were fine between the guys; however, it was too strange when I wanted to go see Pete and hang out while he was bartending. Pete went in, and without an appeal to stay, Aaron happily accepted Pete's two-week notice.

Pete's bartending was only part-time as he was finishing up his master's degree. He planned to work as a high school counselor and had been getting some hours already logged in at a school twenty minutes south of here. The local high school was heavily recruiting him, but he said he wanted some distance from the kids he was helping. He said it wasn't cool to see some of the parents out at a restaurant or bar and know they were a piece of shit, and he needed to refrain from telling them to pay more attention to their kids instead of being out.

Pete stood behind two guys digging in their pockets, counting their cash and finally throwing some on the table. Pete pointed to the door and stood there looming at them before they ran out.

"Just a beer, nothing fancy," Sherrie repeated.

I took the barstool between Sherrie and two retired guys that had just come off the golf course.

Sherrie said, "I don't know what is worse: listening to the old guys complaining about the condition of the course—of course it's gonna be muddy; it's early March, at least they got to play this early in the season—or dealing with Pete right now."

"Are you talking smack about my man?" I laughed. "Why should I order a beer when you have what appears to be a vodka soda?"

"I ordered vodka cranberry."

"Oh. I wonder if has to do with his interaction with Phil." I suddenly felt his warm breath on my check before he gave me a quick kiss.

"Hey," Pete said and walked around behind the bar. Without waiting for me to order, he made me a Baileys and coffee.

"What the hell?" Sherrie protested. "She gets a delightful drink, and I can't even get what I ordered. How do you even knows what she wants? You are going to get yourself fired."

Pete did not even flinch at Sherrie's reaction. "She had a rough day at work, and it's cold out. She is going to want caffeine, something warm, and a little sweet. The bar is out of cranberry juice, and your next order would have been vodka soda. Appreciate the double I pour for you and only charged you for a single."

"Fiancée or not I have to say he schooled you," I said and watched his smile get wide when I said fiancée.

"Why were you so rude to the guys at the end of bar?" Sherrie asked.

"Rude? I was an ass. Just say it." Pete owned up to everything he did and said without hesitation, "They were hitting on the girls sitting behind them and was not getting the hint they were not interested. One guy stumbled out a minute before I told those two they better take care of their friend because they won't be welcomed here any more."

"That's my hero." I beamed.

"What does your boss, Jim, think of your demeanor?" Sherrie asked.

"He prefers it's me instead of him so he can always play the good guy."

"So are you past the whole Phil debacle, or can you give us the details?" I asked.

"I went to buy the cement mix Manuel told me to get."

"Manuel?" Sherrie asked.

Sherrie knew immediately when I answered. "Mr. Green Jeans."

We had given names to the road crew that had been outside the house for two months. Mr. Blue Cowboy would hose down the sidewalk making a clear path for Sherrie on her bicycle. Mr. Red Bandana spent a lot of time in that port-a-potty each morning. Mr. Yellow Vest was always eating something.

I said, "He's been the guy tearing up the street. Monday Pete talked to him about doing a side job for us in the basement."

Pete continued, "I needed him to jackhammer part of the basement floor. When EG converted from the old oil tank heating system, whoever took it out did a poor job on the floor. The cement is raised anywhere from one to four inches

74

and is not even smooth. I am surprised she even bothered to do anything with the floor since she left everything unfinished. The tank sat on metal legs that could have been clipped down. Even the tank is still down there. Removing the floor and pouring fresh cement would have seemed excessive if not finishing the basement, but then again, maybe there were underground pipes I was not aware of."

"Jackhammering! When you were going to tell me?" Sherrie asked.

"Settle down and drink your not vodka cranberry. Why do you think I was asking about your Thursday schedule and when you would be back from the office? I thought I mentioned the jackhammering." I took a long sip of cocktail and realized that I may not have mentioned the noisy work. I did ask about her schedule but didn't consult her about the schedule. I went through the initial plans with her that Pete and I had come up with, but she hadn't been part of the process. I felt my back and armpits go sweaty. It was a micro-step in the beginning of Sherrie not being part of the house. It made me sad.

These past two weeks had been a whirl of emotions and decisions. Being gifted EG's house, the engagement, and immediate house renovations—I'd been so excited about every step forward that I was failing to comprehend how

Sherrie was becoming less involved in my everyday life.

Pete topped of my drink with more Baileys and continued. "Phil was asking what I needed all that stuff for. He made some comment about how that is not the way to repair drywall. I laughed it off and said I was fixing the basement. He freaks out on me again saying I probably don't know what I'm doing. I don't say anything. Then he begins to insist he do it. I say thanks but no thanks. Patty, his wife pops into the conversation saying she was sure EG would be expecting Phil to do it, and it's ok. I told him you and I can handle it. I never mentioned EG does not own the house anymore. None of their business. He mumbled something about EG and stuff I couldn't understand. I started to walk out, and he chased after me. He tried shaking my hand and laughing off his previous comments, but I was done with him and his condescending attitude so I kept walking."

"Who knew an aging one-time peace advocate, antiwar martyr married to a modern day but equally as old hippie can have such a mean streak in him?" I said.

"I got online and ordered everything from the hardware store down in Kirkasaw. If I give you my truck, can you pick it up tomorrow?" Pete asked.

"Can't I take my Jeep? How much is there?"

"It will definitely fit, but it will be dusty."

"Good call. I think I can handle BB?"

"BB?" Pete asked.

"Big Bubba. Your truck," I said.

"I asked if you two ever gave me a nickname, and you said no. Don't tell me you had a secret from me?"

"Again, you never had a nickname, and you know I name cars."

"Don't I get to name my own truck?" Pete asked.

"No," Sherrie and I answered together and laughed.

I asked, "Well, do you have a name for your truck."

We waited for an answer, and I could see the wheels turning.

Pete surprisingly laughed, finally conceding with, "Can't you at least come up with something better than BB?"

"You can't rename something, that's bad luck," Sherrie said.

"That's boats not trucks," Pete said.

The name and not renaming the truck didn't matter because luck ran out.

CHAPTER THIRTEEN

Eleven days after the engagement party.

The lights were bright, the beeping annoying, and the hand was warm and comforting. Pete's voice was shaky but comforting. "It's ok. It's ok. It's gotta be ok."

"I am fine. Just don't let go," I whispered.

"Never," Pete whispered back. While still holding my hand, he jumped up, gave a whoop, and announced, "She is giving orders. All is well."

A hand fell on my shoulder. "Just relax, hon, Don't try to move too much. There are no broken bones. You have a nasty bump on your head, bruise across your chest from the seat belt, and some cuts."

I soon realized the nurse underestimated when she said "some cuts." What I lacked in amount of cuts, I made up for in size and location. Across my left temple, cheek, and neck.

Sherrie and Pete's mom, Peggy, came in the hospital room.

"We heard some shouting," Peggy said.

"She is fine. Some cuts and bruising. No broken bones. Wrist will be sore. Just waking up from the sedative." Pete repeated it several times.

Peggy remained just inside the doorway, and Sherrie scooted around her. She grabbed my toes, and I yelped. Sherrie jumped a foot back, and I tried to laugh but it was more of a sigh.

"So, your foot is not broken, and you still have your twisted sense of humor. All is well. I am outta here," Sherrie said but didn't move.

"Claudia, nice to see you smiling now. I don't want to disturb you while you rest. Gonna head home now." Peggy gave Pete a one-arm hug since he was unable to put both his arms around her while holding my hand. "Pete, come by anytime, and there will be pot roast and potatoes in the refrigerator for you, all of you—better yet, I will have Don bring it to the house."

"Tell Don the door is open," Sherrie said.

"Of course it is. Glad you will be ok, Claudia. Bye."

"Good call since there are few too many people in this room right now. We are waiting for the doctor, but you probably won't have to spend the night here. I will be back in a few." The nurse double-checked some machine I was hooked up to and walked out with Peggy.

I asked Pete, "You called your mom? Anyone else out there? This is kinda embarrassing."

"I didn't call. Marcus did. The 9-1-1 call went to the police station about a truck that went into the ditch, and my name came up with the registration. Wyatt was on duty when the call came in so he called my brother. It wasn't until someone, probably the firefighters, got to the bottom of the ditch and realized it wasn't me. I spoke to your dad. They are headed here."

"Can you tell them that is ok and they don't need to come all the way here?" I asked.

"No way. I can't stop that force of Katie Lyn and Matthew Middleton. If I had to guess, Sherrie is texting them right now that you are fine and your dad probably slowed down to a cool seventy-five miles per hour."

"How did you end up in the ditch?" Sherrie asked.

It was a blur, and bits and pieces were coming back to me. "A car was coming at me, and I had to swerve."

"You didn't hit a deer?" Pete asked.

"No, I don't think so. Didn't see one. I just remember a truck coming at me and the ditch being the best option. I just remember someone screaming. Sorry about BB. How bad is the truck?"

"Don't worry about the truck. Figured it's time to get a new one and name it before you can come up with something crazy."

A knock on the door and in walked friend and officer, Wyatt Baumann. "How are you doing, Claudia?"

"Been better and hoping to go home soon."

"Are you ok to answer a few questions?"

I was surprised when he asked Pete and Sherrie to leave the room. I reviewed my statement with him. Maybe it was the pain meds or the bump on the head, but I found his questions confusing and repetitive. I was saved from more questions when my mom and dad came in.

To be honest, the questions never really stopped—either about me or the incidents.

CHAPTER FOURTEEN

STILL ON THE PORCH.

"Money talk was a not a huge thing for us. Neither one of us has debt. My parents covered my tuition, and I paid for housing and food. I worked the whole time so I came out without owing anything. Living rent-free for two years has been the biggest savings plan I could think of. I had no car payment until a year ago and my parents gifted me the down payment.

"As far as Pete goes, he had some college debt but paid it off shortly after graduating Madison. He worked all through college and for a while afterwards before he took that nine-month backpacking trip through Europe. He came back here after his trip and started his master's program.

He is either in school, working, fishing, or playing baseball," I said.

"So he has tuition, rent, the boat, your weekend bucket list trips, and until recently his truck," Sherrie said.

"That pretty much sums it," I said. "The boat and truck are paid off. He didn't buy them new."

"Let's not forget that ring, wedding, and house renovations that are moving at a rapid pace. Is that you or him paying for everything?" Sherrie, unlike some people in this town, was not questioning Pete's integrity. She was just simply doing math, not her strongest asset. She continued, "I know the lawsuit was about shutting up Phil and not about the money. People in this town see it differently. Money makes people act strange. When people don't have answers, they make up stories and answers."

"I get run down, and then the hardware store blows up. People just assume revenge, lawyers and other shit. We want nothing from them besides peace."

"Just listen to me so you can see what other people see. It doesn't add up. I know how much tuition is, and part-time bartending while doing your master's and getting on-the-job training for minimal pay isn't gonna cover everything. And now what CiCi said about all their rent being covered and the boat slip."

Sherrie and I never had to say "this is between us." It was understood what was said between us stayed between us. This was different because it was not for me to tell. "Can I tell you a secret?"

"You never asked that before. I hope I just didn't offend you by asking about money or questioning Pete's money-handling skills."

"There is not much you can say that will offend me except maybe asking if you have offended me. I know you're just digging for answers; I get it. It's just what I have to share is not my secret. Each year Pete, his brothers, Marcus and Tommy, each receive ten thousand dollars from their parents. It's sorta a pre-inheritance gesture on their part."

"Nice. Every year or just this year?" Sherrie asked.

"The last three or four years."

We sat there watching the sheet curtains blow in the wind, and after slurping noodles, Sherrie said, "That's a lot of money for folks who worked as a factory supervisor and secretary for an insurance company. That maybe puts Pete even. It doesn't add up for his folks. Is there old family money, or is the dad into gambling? Not being sexist, but the mother doesn't seem the type. Don, doesn't either, but of the pair, he is more likely to have a number for a bookie or online account."

I poured the remaining fried rice over the sesame chicken and grabbed a spoon. It was not a time for a fork or chopsticks.

"You might be right, and I hate to admit it," I said. "I have seen his credit statement. His has one main card because he is a points guy. Big-time points guy. Once I filled up the gas tank and didn't add my phone number for rewards because it was below zero out, and I didn't want to spend the extra seconds freezing. When I was filling up the tank, he went inside to grab some windshield wiper fluid, and he slipped on the ice after he paid and he still went back inside to get the points added to my account. I really don't think he has more than two cards. The second card is just a backup and has a zero balance. How did he pay for my ring? I never saw that on the statement. Would he have paid cash?

"Not sure really sure about his family. Dad started college to be an architect but left before he finished and moved here. For one or two winters, they were in Florida, but Peggy missed the boys too much and is hoping for a grandchild soon. I would assume the house is paid for, and as for old family money, I doubt it."

I stood up and started pacing on the porch with beer in hand. Sherrie pulled the blanket over her lap and cuddled with her beer. Evie came out and gave me a hug before collecting the remains of the

Chinese food without saying anything. If I had to guess, she came out to confirm Sherrie's texts that I was doing ok and that I didn't steal her daughter's phone to send out false reports about my well-being.

CHAPTER FIFTEEN

TWELVE DAYS AFTER THE ENGAGEMENT PARTY.

Some things were vivid; others not so much. I expected a sense of relief when I walked out of the hospital. Maybe some cool, fresh air or sunshine raining vitamin D on me, but all I could feel were the three-and-a-half steps to Sherrie's VW Bug.

I realized now that was the start of many conversations starring me without me having a voice in a play about my life.

Sherrie won the argument between her, Pete, and my parents—she would be the one to drive me home from the hospital. My Jeep and dad's truck were too high for me to step up and in. She would be able to find the closest parking spot to our street being the smallest car.

Official report was zero broken bones but severe bruising across my chest. Gash and cuts to the head, neck, and arm, and overall soreness making it difficult and slow moving anywhere. My dad rode in the backseat and hopped out to escort me the half block to our house while Sherrie circled the block looking for a spot to park.

The only instructions from the hospital were rest, rest, eat, and more rest. I was to sleep in any position that made me comfortable. I made it to the living room couch. I tried for the porch sofa, but my dad guided me inside. We were stunned to find my mother heating up soup and making sandwiches. She had left the hospital after me, my dad, and Sherrie.

After my dad positioned me on the couch and adjusted the pillows three times, he covered me with the blanket and went and gave my mom a kiss. They had only last seen each other seventeen minutes ago.

While my mom was driving the family truck back to the house, Mary O'Brien, EG's backyard neighbor—I mean, my backyard neighbor spotted my mom looking for a parking spot. My mom explained why they were in town and Mary offered up their driveway for the night.

My guess because everything was fuzzy for me that she beat us here by a solid four minutes and texted Sherrie to pick up the remaining supplies after having dropped us off. Pete arrived a few minutes later, accepting a beer from my dad and not really leaving the recliner next to me for more than a few minutes until the next morning.

Pete gave me my phone to call work and explain I wouldn't be able to work for two or three days. He promptly took it away after my work call, stating he didn't want me texting or calling anyone with all the pain meds I had taken that night. I learned later he had already called to tell them I wouldn't be in tomorrow, making sure I didn't get into trouble for not calling and not showing up. He was always taking care of me even when I didn't know it, and he still let me handle it as I wanted.

We left it up to Sherrie to text Maddie to give her the proper details so no rumors would start at work about how I came to be in a ditch. I once backed the hotel van into a dumpster, and no one had let me forget it. I had been avoiding a dead raccoon, but it didn't matter as I was the one to put green paint on the new white van.

The next morning, Pete was stiff from sleeping in the recliner all night. My parents stayed in EG's old room and were early risers. My dad went to Peach's the minute it opened while my mom made coffee, bacon, and eggs.

Sherrie was dressed and ready for breakfast by the time hot food was served, and my dad returned with powdered sugar on his sleeve and some warm pastries. Pete brought me coffee, a pastry, and the television remote before he had his first bite. My parents said goodbye right after breakfast and made their way back to the Twin Cities on the condition I should call if I need something that Pete and Sherrie couldn't help with. Pete seemed anxious for them to go.

"You ok with my folks? You're the one that called them," I asked.

"They're great. Its just I got Mr. Green Jeans . . . oh man," Pete said.

"Whats wrong?"

"I just called him Mr. Green Jeans. I have spoken to Manuel everyday, but now I'm starting to talk like you and Sherrie."

"There is nothing wrong with that!" Sherrie shouted and right on cue, a piece of flaky croissant came flying across the room towards Pete. He anticipated the move and swiftly caught it and flung it back at her. "Maybe she does need to move out."

"Back to Manuel. What's that got to do with my parents?"

"Unfortunately, Manuel said he had to do the work in the morning and not this afternoon. I am sure your parents, and of course, I want you to rest. This is going to be loud and annoying. Can I take you to my place? I know it's not as comfortable, but you can sleep in peace. We would

92

have to go now. In a panic, I moved one of my sessions with some students from yesterday afternoon to this morning while I was sitting in the hospital. I'd feel crappy blowing off students twice."

"Sherrie get in here," I yelled, and she bounced into the living room. "Let me tell you both this once as I said to my mom and dad more than once, I AM FINE! Sore but fine. I can handle some jackhammering. The space is not that large."

Pete turned his head towards Sherrie, and they both rolled their eyes at my declaration.

"Maybe I should move out." I laughed. "So now that you two understand I am good, do I have to pay Manuel or did you take care of it?"

"I paid him half. I texted him the back door is open, and I will get him the other half later today if they are still working out front when I get back or tomorrow."

Sherrie left immediately for her job at the leasing office. After Pete had helped me change into different comfy sweats, I promptly fell back asleep on the sofa. I woke up some time later to pounding in my head that was actually just the jackhammering downstairs, but I might as well have been rolling down the embankment all over again.

It thankfully stopped a short time later. Too short of time to be done. Instead of bone-rattling hammering, I heard a chorus of what sounded like a hymn or some type of ceremonial chat and then the back door slamming shut.

Pete texted between meeting with the students and a meeting with the school principal asking how I was doing and what's with Manuel because he got some weird message. I said Manuel was already gone and omitted the stuff about Manuel singing like he was in church. Pete would have thought I'd hit the pain meds too soon again.

When I put my phone down, Jorge knocked and walked in without me telling him to come in. "Are you ok?" His eyes were scanning me and the room. He walked towards the kitchen and then went to the master bedroom and scanned the whole first floor. "Are you ok?"

"I'm fine. Just a little sore from the bruising, and my face, neck, and arms are tender from the cuts."

"He cut you?" Jorge asked "Should I call the police, or Pete? Is Sherrie ok, is she here?"

"What are you talking about?" I asked.

"I just saw someone leave. He was running like he robbed the place."

"What are you doing home? Why are you not at your shop?"

"I got Grandel working at the garage. It's not too busy, and I want to get more work done on my house. Enough about me. What's going on here? Why do you look like hell?"

"The reason for my lovely appearance is that I was in a car accident yesterday. As for who you saw running out of here, Pete hired Manuel to break up the concrete under the previously used oil tank from the old heating system."

Jorge left me on the couch and ran downstairs, and a minute later, he came back up. His work trousers from the knee down and his hands were covered in white concrete dust. "Tell Pete he is going to have to find someone else to finish the job. I doubt Manuel will come back in here. Grandel may do it, if the city doesn't do it for you. He is always looking for extra cash, and I think he has the skills. He'll have to rent the equipment. Is EG in Chicago or off on one of her trips?"

"You know I am right here. Talk to *me* about the house. I tried to sit up, but my movements were slow and slightly painful. Despite what I was telling everyone, I was hurting. I would be fine, but any movement made my skin pull. I had a few stitches because the doctor used some type of surgical glue for less scaring. The slightest twist or tug was painful. Even the light weight of the blanket pressed against the bruises on my chest hurt.

"Stay where you are, Claudia. I wasn't trying to offend you by asking for EG. She just has a deeper history with this place?"

"Place? You make it sound like an industrial building and not our home. Our comfy, homey nest."

Jorge silently nodded and let me continue.

"Just tell me what is going and don't treat me like I can't handle it. I don't need a nurse. I need to know what is happening."

"I'll tell you he didn't run out of here because of a spider." Jorge took the dining room chair, spun it around, straddled it and adjusted his baseball cap before he spoke again. " When Manuel broke through a layer of concrete, he some found human bones."

"Maybe I should call EG," I said.

CHAPTER SIXTEEN

LATER . . . TIME DOESN'T MATTER WHEN IT IS THE WORST DAY EVERY DAY.

The day of the service, everything else was a warm blur. The people, the hugs, the condolences, the suggested ways to move on, the priest mumbling life metaphors. The touching was nonstop: a gentle tap on the arm, hand on the shoulder, full-on embrace, and even a hand on the back guiding me where to be. The nonstop noise and touching was like an anchor in a bottomless ocean.

These days, it was the smell that haunted me. If I managed to sleep, I woke to the smell. It didn't last long, and I didn't know where it came from. After the smell, I saw the coffin and felt claustrophobic.

The church had some saint attached to it, but I didn't need to know who as it was not my church and I had no reason to go back. The day we planned the service, Pete's parents, Don and Peggy, and I walked into the lower level of the church to an open hall. Metal chairs were stacked along one wall and tables on another. The scent was a blend of stale, forced heat, damp linoleum floors, burnt coffee, and foot powder.

Pete's sister-in-law, Rachel, who was married to his older brother, Thomas, came downstairs to tell us Father William and everyone else was in a conference room off the narthex. We had come from the funeral home where we picked out a temporary casket and wrote the obituary notice, which nearly broke Peggy.

Marcus was upset at the idea of a church funeral and the luncheon afterwards that his mother laid out. He wanted a celebration of life that was just short of a fraternity party. Marcus argued Pete hadn't stepped into a church in a decade unless it was to attend a wedding or funeral and that holidays don't count either.

Peggy said, "I didn't get a church wedding. I am getting a funeral. You can party some other time. A time to gather and be lead by our faith." It was raw emotion. She was visibly shaking, and Don reached out and held her as she buried her head in her hands.

Marcus then turned his attention to me.

I said, "I can't, not now. The church is fine."

Marcus looked to Thomas who remained silent.

Rachel spoke for her and Thomas, "We're ok with whatever you all decide."

Peggy conceded to Pete being cremated after the funeral, and we agreed on a headstone and the urn to place there at a later time.

Rachel and Peggy both had on sweaters. Peggy had her arms wrapped around herself when she wasn't holding Don's hand. I, however, had sweat rolling down my neck, and my arms were clammy. The beige walls of the little room off the narthex seemed to leaning in on me. We internalized our grief differently.

Peggy and the priest did most of the talking. I could feel everyone breathing and it sucked the breathe out of me. When it came time to discuss the luncheon I felt something nudge my elbow.

I looked back and no one was there. "Please let me plan the menu and take care of those arrangements."

Peggy was too exhausted to argue and just said I should speak with Mary Ann at Reyem's. Pete's mom had some serious skills at navigating a situation as a place had not been previously decided. I guess raising three good, honest, and respectful boys, one must have mothering skills I didn't know about. I didn't think about going anywhere else.

On the way out, Marcus stopped and wanted to make sure beer would be available, and if he had to fund it, he would make it happen. Peggy was still talking to the priest when Don came over and said to add an extra twenty or so to the headcount on top of whoever is at church. Usually, someone from the funeral home would call the restaurant with a headcount for the buffet. Some of the guys from the plant couldn't be at the service and would attend the luncheon. However, I should minus two because he didn't expect his brother, Pete's uncle, to stay for the luncheon.

Then it was Rachel's turn. She apologized for the comment Peggy made at the funeral home. "She was directing her anger at Thomas and me. While she is a loving and wonderful mother-in-law, you really can't ask for anyone better, sometimes she wills some of her opinions sharply. She never got over the fact we held our wedding in a park and not in the church. Your service was a wonderful job, and considering the circumstances, she couldn't passively suggest or comment about your choice of venue or priest."

"It's pastor, not priest. He is a Lutheran minister, so we address him as pastor," I said.

That was a lot of Morris family information I didn't need to absorb. I excused myself when I

100

saw my mom and dad were in the last pew of the empty sanctuary.

I hadn't asked them to come, but they figured I might need a moment away from Pete's family that was grieving as much as I was.

"We left the diner and decided to walk around for a bit. We saw you and Peggy and Don come in here. We weren't sure long you would be, so we just stopped in for a minute.

"I need to go plan the meal," I said.
They did not offer to do it for me or suggest how it should be done. They were my rock, my pillar, and everything I needed at the moment. They treated me like an adult that just needed support and were not pushing their grief onto me.

CHAPTER SEVENTEEN

TWELVE DAYS AFTER THE ENGAGEMENT PARTY - STILL THE MORNING AFTER MY ACCIDENT.

I texted EG to call when she had some time available. I had no idea what part of her England, Guernsey Island, and France trip she was on and if she even had cell service while hiking. She had called Sunday during the surprise engagement party to say congratulations. The call lasted all of forty seconds since there was a line of people waiting to talk to me and of course to take the phone and talk to EG.

Not wanting to panic EG, I added to the text it was basic questions about the house but needed to be answered fairly fast.

Jorge had gone back to his house for a bit before he headed to his shop. We didn't say much to each other after I confirmed with my own eyes what was in the basement. We silently agreed to wait to hear from EG before we took any action.

EG's reply came two hours later.

> Poor cell service on the trails.
> Might be able to call tonight or after
> tomorrow's hike
> Remember six hour time difference
> Send me your questions

I rolled off the couch at ten thirty for lunch. I picked pieces of lettuce out of a bag and dipped them in dressing while I waited for the cornflake potato casserole to heat up. While I ate, I tried coordinating Pete's and Sherrie's schedules for them to be home at the same time. This was too much for me to do on my own, and it didn't feel right to tell one and not the other.

Decided to send EG one more text.

> Removing the old oil drum and have
> foundation issues.

Next, I called my mom at work. I thought she might have some knowledge of the house or maybe remember who EG had bought it from, but she didn't have much to tell me. She said she would think about it and call me tonight. Then it was

endless questions about how I was feeling, so I
drew that conversation to a quick close.

CHAPTER EIGHTEEN

Back on the porch with Sherrie.

I picked up the box CiCi had brought over. I pulled out the photo books Rachel, Pete's sister-in-law, had made for Pete from his mostly solo backpacking trip through Europe. To keep his mother from worrying too much, he sent a couple of pictures a day. Rachel took the photos from Peggy's phone and made the souvenir books. I had gone through the books before with Pete. He had been in some amazing places—Paris, Amsterdam, Berlin, Munich, Innsbruck, Prague, Budapest, and some city in Romania before heading finally Switzerland and the Alps.

Sherrie flipped through one of the books, and I took the other. "He's not much of a photographer. Food pics and odd building shots are most of them," she said.

"These are only the pictures he sent his mom. Each time he changed cities, he would take a photo from the view from his youth hostel, hotel, or Airbnb to show her he was not in a bad neighborhood and that he was eating properly. You think Rachel could have edited some of this before printing the books. This may have been more of a gift for Peggy than it was for Pete," I said.

Sherrie flipped through the pages and noted, "He's not in many photos. Who are all the kids in these pics? Is that one Pete?" She pointed to a group of kids smiling in a dusty field between two chairs with a battered soccer ball in front of them and a very skinny Pete behind them.

"You know he is not one for selfies, and they were to satisfy his mother. The kid pics are from when he was in Romania. He went to a small village with an orphanage. Somehow, he ended up staying for several weeks helping repair some of the buildings. His dad even went over and helped. Don stayed in the village for seven days before they trotted off somewhere else. I think that place hit him hard, seeing all those kids. It was part of his decision to get his master's and become a school counselor."

"What's this?" Sherrie held up a business card that dropped from the back page and said,

"Cade Whitmore, Accountant. With an area code from the Madison area. Who is this dude?"

"No idea. Not even sure it's Pete's." I picked up two textbooks from the box. They had been on Pete's dresser as long as I had known him. I was not even sure from what class, semester, or year they were from. My elbow pinched again, causing me to drop the books back in the box. A second card fell out, and this one read Gunner L. Driver. This card was thicker than the business card. I threw the books on top of the card. I didn't want Sherrie to see it. There were too many questions already, and now why did Pete have this credit card with Gunner L. Driver on it? I knew it belonged to Pete.

CHAPTER NINETEEN

A WEEK AFTER MY ACCIDENT.

"I never expected to see you two run in here. Unless you're are checking in, step aside, and let this couple past you. Wyatt, don't you dare walk too far in with those muddy boots. Sherrie, don't you have your study group?" I said.

Without missing a nanosecond, Sherrie took charge, "I guess I'm skipping it. Maddie, can you check them in so Claudia can come with us? Claud, grab your purse and let's go."

"Whats going on?" I slowly stepped out from behind the front desk of the hotel. I was working Wednesday evening. Actually, I was working a lot of evenings and days lately. Since I'd missed several days because of my accident I was covering for everyone who wanted time off. Sometimes, being a salaried manager doesn't pay off. "Whats up?"

"Wyatt refused to tell me until we are together. He nearly drove me off the road," Sherrie said.

"I didn't run you down. I pulled over ahead of you, and you freaked out." Wyatt turned to me and said, "Please grab your purse and whatever and get in the truck with me."

"You're kinda freaking me out." I stood shoulder to shoulder with Sherrie, both of us staring at Wyatt.

"I wanted to make sure I did right this time. Unlike last time when his parents were called and it was you in the accident. There's been another accident."

"Hell's bells." Sherrie and I chorused.

"I'm off duty, but I heard the sirens and made some calls. I went to find you and saw Sherrie on her bike and knew she should be with you. It's Pete. Pete's been transported to the hospital."

Silence floated from me, and ice went down my spine.

CHAPTER TWENTY

Two Days after Jenna and Kay brought us dinner and told us about the town becoming divided.

Sherrie and I were sitting across from Jenna and Kay when I asked, "Why are we in the most uncomfortable booth in the town?"

Kay answered, "Privacy. These high-back wooded booths prevent people from giving us the stare down. And, I was craving one of Bumbles' burgers."

"I'm glad you were able to join us. What's the update on Pete?" Jenna asked.

"I was sitting with Pete when you guys texted and the thought of Bumbles food made him perk up. Although it just might be fries, not much appetite for anything else. He is restless when he's awake. Sleeping a lot. Right now, it's all about the fever the doctors can't control. The broken and cracked ribs will eventually be fine. The burns are still gross, but thankfully, they can treat them without transferring him to a burn unit. Oh, the sprained ankle is healing nicely since he can't get out of the hospital bed."

"How are his parents doing?" Kay asked.

"They are pretty sold. I mean raising three boys, I am sure they have been through some broken bones and a few hospital visits. Once we got the all clear on no head injuries, we all seemed to relax a bit. Peggy keeps making lists of things Pete needs, everything from socks to vitamins. When not making a list, she is knitting. Don't know if she is actually kitting anything in particular or just needing to do something with nervous energy. His dad is easy to talk with. We can touch on any subject easily without it being forced.

"I appreciate the fact that he immediately made it so I could receive all the medical information. God, that hospital takes that stuff seriously. Marcus isn't on the list so he has been texting me and calls for updates after he speaks with his mom just to make sure he has all the information. His mom and I actually laugh at it. Follow up with Thomas and Rachel who come in together every evening at five fifteen for forty-five minutes. Thomas returns after dinner until ten or eleven."

"How are you holding up?" Jenna asked.

"I swing between exhaustion and adrenaline. Work has been fine adjusting my hours, but that grace period is running short. I can manage that as long as the hourly employees don't hit overtime making up for my absence. Earlier this week, I was stuck making beds to cover for the housekeeping supervisor and two people called off sick. Sick! I would like to show them sick." I closed my eyes and leaned back in the booth.

"While she cat naps. I can tell you central air guys finally managed to get the new unit to the house. I don't know how, but it's sitting on the driveway."

"So you'll be able to get it installed this week?" Kay asked.

"Probably not. Had to put it on hold. The basement renovation is . . ." Sherrie took a long drink before she skirted around about the problem we'd discovered in the basement. "We have to get someone to look at the duct work."

I think I dozed off because the next thing I knew, a bowl of chili that I hadn't ordered was sitting in front of me with extra cheese loaded up on top.

"Sorry about that. I guess I was tired," I said.

"Don't worry. We invited you here for a break from hospital not to entertain us," Kay said.

We were all quietly eating when a group sat in the booth behind Sherrie and me. It was painful and educational listening to them.

Male one: "I heard he was mad and wanted to give it to the old guy. Torch the place. That would shut me up."

Female one: "There is no way he lit the place up on purpose. I know Pete, that's not his style. It's a hardware store. I'm surprised it doesn't happen more often with all the crap they have for sell."

Kay, Jenna, and Sherrie all had their eyes on me. I mouthed the words, "I'm fine."

Male one: "You push anyone, and you don't know what they will do. I have seen him kick people out of the bar."

Male two: "Hey, dumbass, isn't that part of his job as bartender and bouncer? I heard they had Phil arrested for trespassing, breaking and entering or something like that."

Female one: "So Pete decided to notch it up, torch the place, and then go back in?"

Male one: "Are you sure he went back in? Maybe he was just trapped."

Male two: "There is a witness that saw him come out and then go back in."

Male one: "Maybe he wanted a bigger explosion and went back to set something else off

116

or realized he dropped his wallet or something. Isn't there an arrest pending?"

Male two: "I heard he saw someone inside or maybe he wasn't finished robbing the place before it went up for the final time."

Female one: "If they had Patty arrested for running her off the road, they would be one up, so no need to burn down the place."

Male two: "We could be missing a step in between."

Female one: "I would torch or blow away anyone coming at me with their vehicle. That includes both of you."

Uncomfortable laughter from the two males.

Male one: "How many lawsuits are there between them? Insurance money. Hospital bills can't be cheap."

Male two: "What about the car accident? Didn't Phil save Claudia and call the ambulance?"

Female two: "You boys are worse than high school girls gossiping. Get the story straight. She was run off the road."

Male one: "She was avoiding a deer. I would have taken that deer head-on. Imagine if it still had its rack on it. Easiest kill of the season, legit too even out of hunting season."

Male two: "No way, dude, you won't let anything get near that truck of yours, not even a twelve-point buck. You would have swerved and squealed like a pig if a leaf landed on the hood."

Female one: "My cousin was in the truck behind Claudia and said he didn't see any deer. Doesn't mean there wasn't one. And Aaron said it was no swerve but a direct aim for Claudia. If you are gonna talk, get the story right, it wasn't Phil driving, it was his wife, Patty. Aaron also said that he couldn't see everything, but the—"

Rose: "Whatya folks want to order?"

Male one: "Whats your take on—"

Rose: "I got no take on anything. You gonna order or waste the space?"

After Rose took their orders, it continued.

Male two: "It's the money thing. I expect they are thinking of a big payout soon, but I would think Pete knows these things take time."

Female one: "Why soon? Did you hear him say something?"

Male two: "I was talking to Dena. She was working when he came in shopping for a central air unit. There was no hesitation with price on the unit and installation. Even tried to speed up install day. He threw the whole thing on his credit card and skipped the no financing we offer. All in a house that is not his. She must be an ace in bed if that dude is dropping that kind of money."

Female one: "You don't have a clue about them. Did you ever consider EG is paying as it is

118

her house, and Pete is just helping with getting it installed before summer? I am assuming EG doesn't have to worry about money. Can you image all this time and no central air-conditioning?"

We finished eating in silence when Kay was about to say something, and I stopped her, "It's fine. Good to hear it fresh."

Rose dropped off our check and a to-go order of double fries for Pete that Sherrie must have ordered when she ordered me my chili. Before Rose stepped away, she said, "Not sure where you all are parked, but the back door to the alley is unlocked. It will save you a few steps, otherwise through the front door is just fine by me."

"What was that all about? Giving us directions?" Kay spoke softly as did the rest of us, not wanting to let our neighbors on the other side of the booth know who we are.

Sherrie answered, "She wants us to know we don't have to walk out in front of everyone in the restaurant. She understands if we want privacy or to confront everyone gossiping."

"I think she is hoping you walk out front. She is staying behind the bar watching us," Jenna said.

"Oh, how sweet," Sherrie said.

"Why? Because she is looking for bruhaha and wants a front-row seat?" I said.

Sherrie replied, "Not that. But admit it, ladies, we would all be waiting and watching." We all nodded in agreement. "Rose didn't charge for the extra cheese on Claud's chili. That's her way of giving you support."

Jenna went to the bar with our credit cards and signed for everyone. Her and Kay left through the front door and Sherrie and I out the back door, leaving everyone to keep their gossip flowing free that night.

CHAPTER TWENTY-ONE

Back on that porch.

I'd really thought I'd known him. If I had to guess, most people who had been dating a year and were engaged would have said that too, but things were just easy with us. There was never a second thought about sharing our phone passwords, talking about dating history or all the girls that hit on him while he was bartending. There was no hesitation or drama. Weekends with the guys fishing or me with the girls shopping and dancing in the cities never produced jealousy or the feeling of being left out.

We talked about our careers and where we might want to live and how long we wanted to stay in River Bend. Building our dream cabin in the mountains. City, suburbs, or rural communities, he would always be able to find a job, and I was flexible on where my hotel career could take me. We wanted to stay in River Bend for the near future and both loved our community we had around here.

Now, there was a gaping hole that Gunner L. Driver was digging deeper. I didn't have to Google the name. It was Pete. There was no doubt in my mind that this credit card was Pete's. Gunner was the real name of the dog from the movie *The Sandlot*, and Donald Driver was his second-favorite Packer. It was the card that fell from the old textbook from Pete's dresser that CiCi had brought over. There was this other side of him he'd never shared. Why have a secret credit card?

Secrets, I agree, Pete, they suck.

CHAPTER TWENTY-TWO

THE EVENING AFTER MY ACCIDENT.

Five hours after sending EG the message, I woke up on my bed drooling. Still in my salad-dressing-soaked sweatshirt, dazed and confused. No lights were on in my room or upstairs. Noises were coming from downstairs or outside. It was hard to tell who was talking and where it was coming from.

My body was still aching, and my head was foggy like a double dose of nighttime cough syrup followed up with a shot of whiskey.

My phone had numerous messages and missed calls from Pete and a few texts from Sherrie and my parents. Pete was stuck at the high school until six. Sherrie was staying on campus until late unless I needed something.

I had to sit up so I could shift my flour-sack body of dead weight. I'd been sleeping on one of the pill containers. The lid popped off, and pills were scattered across the bed. Counting the sleeping pills, I realized I must have taken two of them by mistake.

My phone beeped again. It was Sherrie asking if I was alive.

I looked at Pete's location, and it showed him twenty-five minutes from home. I had no idea who was in the house. I texted Jorge asking if he had come back or if he sent Grandel to look at the project. I laughed to myself when I said "project." Saying bones, was too much.

He replied immediately they were both at the shop. My head was still fogged over, and without really thinking about what might happen, I just simply stated someone's in the house. Failure set in when I tried standing up. My body ached, and my head felt lopsided and heavy. I remember reaching for the nightstand, but my hand only went as far as my pillow, and then my head followed and I was out again.

I woke up to Pete sitting on the bed, rocking me by my shoulders, and Wyatt standing over us.

"Claud, Claud, Claud?" Pete's voice was shaky.

"I'm up. I'm here."

Pete helped me sit up. His embrace touched every bruise from the car accident, but I didn't want to pull away.

"Why were you not answering your phone? Are you ok? Jorge called. Are you ok?"

"Get me some water," I said.

Pete handed me an old water bottle from the dresser.

"Whats going on? Something wrong, Wyatt?" I said.

"I was hoping you could tell us."

The water erased some of the cotton mouth. My mind was slow to start. I drank more water to buy some time. "I took a long nap."

"I got a call from Jorge saying there is someone in your house, so I came to check it out," Wyatt said.

"That's right. I guess I came upstairs, fell asleep, and woke up to noises. I heard voices. Sherrie had texted she was still on campus, and Pete was driving. I just asked if it was him, and I guess I fell asleep again."

"I cleared the first floor, basement, and was headed upstairs when Pete came in. I can't believe I have to say this again to you, will you please start locking your doors? EG has to change her ways," Wyatt said.

Pete didn't correct him. I am very proud of the gift EG had given me, but I don't need to show it off, and Pete understands that.

We heard Jorge's motorcycle ride onto his driveway outside my bedroom window. "Pete, tell him you and Wyatt are here, and he should come over later."

"Does he need to come over at all?" Pete asked as he typed.

"You searched the whole house and found nothing?" I asked.

"Claud, I know how to do a house search." Wyatt stood with his hands on his hips, looking from me to Pete.

"Ok then. Thanks for coming," I said.

"You take it easy with those pain meds. No driving but I am sure you know that," Wyatt said.

"It's not the pain meds. I think I took too many sleeping pills," I said.

"You don't need to explain that you were out. It took me a minute to wake you. We can let Wyatt go?"

"Hate to know Wyatt thinks I don't know my drugs." I tried laughing, but it sounded like I was whining.

"My eyesight is pretty good, and I can tell you that's for pain and not sleep." Wyatt was looking at the plastic pill container I had in my hand.

Pete stood up. "I think we got it figured out now. Thanks for your help, Wyatt."

I needed to defend my error. "I just probably carried the bottle upstairs in case I needed some pain meds. Too many would make me loopy not tired, right?"

"No idea. I am no doctor, just your average cop."

"Wyatt, totally appreciate you coming over here and taking care of this. Let me walk you out. Claud, are good here for a minute?" Pete stepped into the doorway and waited for Wyatt.

"I am just going to use the bathroom, and I'll be down," I said.

Pete helped me up, and the boys walked downstairs together.

After I peed and threw cold water on my face, I switched sweatshirts and went downstairs. Pete was at the front door looking out to the street. I walked over and put my arms around him the best I could with my bruising. "What was your rush to get rid of Wyatt? Do I smell or something?"

"Jorge was texting and asking who was here and if you found out anything and if you were okay since you haven't answered any of his texts. I understood that to mean something went on here, and we probably shouldn't talk in front of Wyatt— Cop Wyatt or Friend Wyatt."

All I could do was nod in agreement. I rubbed the sand out of my eyes.

Pete said, "From Jorge's call earlier after you told him someone was here, he called me and said something was up but wouldn't go into it on the phone. I didn't want to ask too many questions with Wyatt here. If something was wrong, you'd have told Wyatt. So what's up?"

"It's one of the reasons I love you. You just knew to cover for me without questioning or accusing me of something. You got my back."

"Of course I got your back—you got a cute ass."

I laughed, kissed him, and added, "And a heart for you."

"Geez, can you two just stop being so adorable and gross. You gotta warn a girl when you are gonna get mushy. Are you guys trying to make me move out faster now?" Sherrie was bringing her bike onto the front porch.

"Thank you for skipping study group," I said.

"Honestly, not so much for you as it was the break in the weather. I wanted to get me and my bike out of the rain before it gets worse. I haven't been out much yet this year, and my legs aren't up to speed. Pun intended."

I still was erasing my midday slumber when I said, "Alrighty, letsh get Jorge here so we only have to do repeat twis once."

"You okay? You're talking like your tongue is glued to the roof of your mouth." Sherrie left her wet windbreaker on the porch and held open the door for Jorge.

Pete and Sherrie held their questions as Jorge and I led them to the basement, but we were the ones speechless when we discovered the bones were gone.

CHAPTER TWENTY-THREE

A DAY AFTER I MOVED OFF THE PORCH AND THREE DAYS BEFORE THE FIRE AT THE RIVER.

My mom had gone to have a drink with an old friend. Sherrie was out somewhere. Earlier that morning, I'd spoken with my boss, telling her I'd be back to work on Monday. I was somewhere in the middle of the seven stages of grief. I had pamphlets from the funeral home, a leaflet from the church, and a few books from the well-meaning supporters, but I had no interest in understanding where I was. Shock, Denial, Anger, Bargaining, Depression, Acceptance, and Processing. Did it really matter what stage?

Something was stirring inside my head.

At least now I was able to focus on something. I wasn't dwelling on missing him. I was able to focus on the missing piece.

I had spent most of my time on the patio. The last few days, the house had felt crowded. If I had a return date to work, maybe that would provide relief for our parents and Sherrie.

She had been a solid rock through all this. She said earlier that our parents where here for me and her. I also knew she had been away a lot. I never asked how she was doing. I am not the only one who lost Pete. He was a friend to many and of course to Sherrie. She was being a supportive friend that has thoroughly been then there for me, and I just unintentionally yet greedily soaked up all the pity, sympathy, empathy, and didn't once think beyond my own feelings.

I realized that she'd had someone on our couch, someone else's coffee brand, someone else's stuff on the counter. The beloved supporters were also cracking our routine of a three, now back to to a two-person household.

If I showed signs of activity, maybe Sherrie and I could get the house to ourselves and maybe find an old routine. I owed her that much.

I received endless messages of support, and I responded to very few of them. Some, I had no idea who it was or how they'd gotten my number. One message came three days after the funeral. It was from an area code in southeast Wisconsin, with a simple text:

Ben Butler.

Deep down I knew that that message would be the answer. I wanted answers. Everyone wanted answers, although I didn't care what everyone wanted. Something was holding me back from connecting with whoever sent the message. Why did someone else know what was going on? Was I being set up?

CHAPTER TWENTY-FOUR

The four of us stood looking at the fresh cement. Absent were skeletal bones, canvas bag, and cement dust Jorge and I had seen earlier.

"Explain it again. What you said as we walked down the stairs. Manuel came here, started drilling, and from what you can tell, freaked out and ran out of here. You and Jorge came down and saw a body?" Pete wasn't really doubting me but more or less confirming the wild thoughts in his head.

Jorge softly answered for both of us, "Um, ah, yes."

Pete and Sherrie probably would have believed just one of us, but it would have taken a lot of explaining. It was comforting to have Jorge weirded out like I was. I was weak to begin with, and my knees barely held me up. Pete steadied me with his hand on my back. Sherrie stood with her hands on her hips waiting for the punchline. I reached out and grabbed Jorge's forearm. He was frozen as I was shaky.

"I don't get it. I don't get it. I really don't get t. How? Why?" No one answered me. "Was I that out of it? How did this happen? Jorge, you saw it right?"

"Without a doubt."

"Somebody was here. Did Manuel come back?"

Pete was on his phone and typing away, and after what was probably only thirty seconds and not thirty minutes, Pete finally said, "It was not Manuel. He left, not coming back inside. Something about bad juju and giving back what we paid him. He will only say something if we ask."

"Say something?" I asked.

"Like when we call the police," Sherrie said.

"NO! Oh, god. No." It was my gut instinct that answered. "I need to talk to EG first. Besides what are we gong to say, someone broke in and cemented over some old bones?"

"Ah, yes! That is exactly what you say," Sherrie said.

"Hmph, my first lesson in owning a home is that sometimes it sucks," I said and smacked my tongue to the roof of my mouth for the twentieth time. The medicine gave me cotton mouth.

Pete bent down, and with the back of his hand, touched the patched area. "It's still wet."

Jorge suddenly pulled me towards the doorway and was reaching for Sherrie when he said, "Watch it, Pete. I don't think that white stuff is concrete dust or drywall dust. It's probably lye."

Sherrie slipped between the wooden studs that until two days ago held up the drywall for the tank room. Jorge stepped over the rubble Manny had just created this morning. He also stepped over a bag of quick-dry cement. Pete took my hand, and we walked up stairs.

I flicked on some lights in the kitchen and living room. With the rain clouds and after my daylong blackout nap, I really had no idea what time it was.

Sherrie repeated herself for the third time, "Bones, no bones? Can you two start from the beginning? Wait, I think I need a beer for this."

Jorge resumed his position from this morning, straddling the dining room chair. Pete covered me with a blanket and sat next to me on the sofa, holding his beer and my root beer. Sherrie pulled a large fleece blanket over her as she settled in the reclining chair and asked me to start at the beginning.

"You know the first part, but let's review it anyway," I said.

"How do I know the beginning?" Sherrie asked.

"Didn't I tell you? On the phone? I swear I talked to someone. Maybe I dreamt it." I tried rubbing my temples, but the fresh wounds stopped me. "My head feels so heavy."

"When you mix up sleeping pills and pain pills you are bound to feel funny," Pete said.

"The funny thing is I don't remember taking any pills. Just drinking stuff."

"I guess that is the sign of some good meds." Sherrie laughed.

Jorge and I recounted the morning. Pete and Sherrie didn't interrupt and had few questions. I mean what could they ask that we would have answers to?

"This morning, Manuel jackhammered until he saw human remains. Jorge and I also saw them. Now the corner of the basement where the old oil tanker stood had a fresh layer of cement."

"Did EG say anything last week? Something about the house. I don't even know what she would say. 'Here's the house, with a body but don't worry about it.' Sherrie half laughed.

"It is pretty much as I had said. She gifted me the house then worried she was giving me an old house that may need a lot of work."

"How long has she had the house?" Jorge asked.

"She was able to buy it shortly after college with the advancement for her first book and writing for some magazine so just over twenty years. Not bad for a single lady in her twenties back then."

"Amen," sang Sherrie. "I don't need a house I would settle for a weekend in London."

"She lived here for about a year before she met a Duncan. He was a graduate student from somewhere in Scotland. They were married eight months after they met. He died in a car crash on an icy night on Route 29 outside of town less than a year into their marriage.

"She has had boyfriends on and off since then. No one else officially lived in the house as far I can remember. About ten years ago, she bought her condo in Chicago and has been splitting her time when not traveling."

Sherrie was reclining in the chair, looking at the ceiling as I spoke, and peeling the label off her beer bottle. "Was there any . . . ? Did you see some . . . ? What about . . . ? You said it was what looked like the ribcage, spine, arm, and maybe a shirt or some cloth fibers. Anything to help narrow down time frame? Before you respond don't answer my inane questions. I am sure you would have said something."

"We, at least I, didn't dig around or move anything," I said.

Jorge also answered, "When I first went to the basement, it was pretty much as it is now. The room with the old oil tank had the door off its hinges, and it was leaning against the far wall. The big garbage can with the busted-down drywall, I think was in the center of room and not near the washing machine, but I can't be too sure about that. The bags of ready-mix cement were unopened in the corner. Didn't think I would need to recount the layout of a tomb."

I couldn't stop shivering. Pete asked if I wanted something hot to drink, and I opted for some hot chocolate. When he stood up, I lost my counterbalance and spilled some of his beer he gave me to hold.

Pete came back into the living room and tossed me a kitchen towel and said, "I found some hot chocolate, but it looks to be kinda old."

"It's probably been here since my brother and I came to visit when we were in grade school. I'll take some soup my mom made yesterday and some cheesy potatoes."

"That sounds good. I'll help." Sherrie sprang from the recliner and helped me up.

Jorge followed us to the kitchen island declining any food.

"Are you sure you don't want anything, Jorge? These are the good cheesy potatoes Katie Lyn made."

For the past year or so, Sherrie and I had been eating carbs like a biker and runner respectively in their early twenties. You could always find mashed potatoes or our favorite, the cornflake-hash brown-cheese potatoes some call funeral potatoes. We started experimenting with different versions. Ranch seasoning was just ok; diced-up broccoli was a split decision with Sherrie voting yes and me a sold no. The all-time favorite was Sherrie's secret recipe. The secret had only lasted nine hours when divulging she had added pureed carrots.

Settling around the kitchen island and doing the mundane things like getting silverware and plates gave each of us a moment to realign our thoughts of what we just saw.

While Pete heated up the giant soup kettle on the stove, he asked, "Why are we not calling the police right now? Would she knowingly pass on a house with a body in it? Someone came into this house clearly knowing what was down there. They either took it away or probably dumped lye all over it to destroy what was left. It would be too much to continue to dig and then haul it away."

Sherrie slid a plate of potatoes she had just microwaved over to me.

I stared at the fork in my hand, and a tear fell from my cheek. "Maybe it's the meds talking as to why I am so emotional, but look at everything here. EG just didn't give me a house. She gave me a house full of house stuff. There are towels, a chair, cheese grater, measuring spoons. Geez, I have a washer and dryer, a garage for my car, and that porch." More tears fell. "She gave me everything in it and all of you. She gave me life with my parents and gave me a community. This house is our home. Maybe this is what I owe her. Someone gives you one birthday or a Christmas gift and you say thank you, but how many thank-yous equal a home. Someone could be protecting EG. Just let me talk to her before we call the police."

"That's a pretty good argument," Sherrie said.

Pete stayed at the stove, and with the wet ladle waving in the air towards me, he said, "Fine, but that is the last time you get to tear up to win an argument."

Jorge went to the fridge, retrieved another beer, and said something inaudible, causing Pete to laugh and say, "Guilty."

Jorge finally said what was gnawing at the back of everyone minds but didn't have the emotion, logic, or guts to say, "So we don't think it's Duncan down there?"

Sherrie jumped in first. "There is no way. He died in a auto accident. Right?"

"That is what I have been told all my life. Why would she gift me a dead body house?"

"That might be the best way to unload the house if she knew. She might never have expected you to tear up the basement within a week of having the house," Jorge said. " She probably expected you two to stay a few years and sell it."

"Again, we are assuming she knows about the bones," I said. "We don't know how long that person has been there."

"Why do you think she never finished the space down there?" Jorge said. "I once asked if she wanted my help. I'd said I could do it cheaper and probably better than most contractors in this town. She flat out declined any sort of conversation about the project."

Pete piped in, "She is a single lady and maybe just didn't need the additional space completed. EG knowing or not knowing may not matter at this point. She is overseas and has no clue what we're doing. You are all over looking the fact that someone knows we are digging down there and wants it hidden. How could they do that without getting caught?"

"Mr. O'Brien, behind us here, is a former Milwaukee detective. He'd know how to watch the house. What's his connection to the house is beyond me," Sherrie said.

"That cement flooring was like that as long as I can remember. When we would visit as kids that basement would freak me out because it was unfinished, dark, and damp. O'Brien's have been here maybe ten years," I said.

"I really don't think it's Mr. O'Brien. Just tossing random ideas out there. This is so odd. Claud, you really didn't hear anything?"

"I was out of it. I don't even remember going upstairs. If there was no more jackhammering, there wouldn't be much noise. I just thought I talked to you."

CHAPTER TWENTY-FIVE

A FEW MONTHS DOWN THE LINE - SOMEONE ELSE'S STORY.

Listening to Claudia talk baby names was one of the most special things I have witnessed in my lifetime. There would be no better mother for him. She experienced such grief, managed to pull herself out of it, and now has the most precious thing in the world.

I might not be around to watch him grow up, but I know he will be loved and cherished.

CHAPTER TWENTY-SIX

My phone was blowing up with text messages and calls. I finally answered Mia's. "I should be there in twenty if no cops are out. I gotta make one stop."

"One stop? Are you crazy? Do you do know how many people are starting to show up? Whoever you have to talk to next is probably on their way here, or they don't want to talk to you. I don't think you have to worry about the police. Most of them are here. Marcus is going nuts. At first, he was having fun telling people what to do, but having too many questions and conflicting answers has him in a tailspin. Sherrie is insisting they wait for you to start the bonfire, but Marcus is ready to burn down the whole area."

"How long has Sherrie been there? How does she look?" I was nervous waiting for Mia to answer.

I couldn't have Pete's celebration of life without her. I couldn't do the next few months without her. We were tired. Everyone was. She and I needed a break from all of this. For a whole day, she hadn't gotten out of her pajamas earlier this week. I never thought she wouldn't not be at Pete's celebration of life bonfire, but I wanted her there fully ready to celebrate the spirit and goodwill Pete had always projected. I would later learn she was always with me, and because of her I always had someone to be at my side.

Mia was out of breath when she talked. "She looks good. The cast on her arm is drawing a lot of questions, and the pothole her bike hit is getting bigger each time she retells the story. By the time you get here, it will be the size of the hole in the road in front of your house."

"Not surprised. I just need to see someone, and then I will be there. If Marcus is going too nuts, stick Peggy on him if she is there. I'm still not sure she approves of the party or not."

"She is here, and you won't believe what she brought. I think she is finally on board with celebrating and not mourning. I should wait until

148

you get here to tell you this as it might make you tear up and drive off the road."

"Seriously! Now you are going to start editing what and when I'm told stuff. I can handle it." I slowed down to seventy-five miles an hour on the fifty-five mile an hour county road. I had cruise control on for the first hour of the drive on the interstate. Ms. Ada Jones had made sure I was ok before I left the office, but nothing could really prepare me for the next phase.

All I could focus on was that I was done with secrets, surprises, lawsuits, finding the truth, lawyers, lawyer offices, and NDAs. Well, maybe not done with a secret and Law.

"What are you saying?" Mia was practically yelling. I could hear the wind and voices in the background. "NDAs what? What are you signing now? I thought you were done with all the legal stuff. Forget that I asked that. I understand the point of nondisclosure agreement."

I snapped back to my conversation with Mia, "Not NDAs. I was saying done with the DA's office and lawyers." I didn't know why I had to lie especially when she'd just said she understands the point of not discussing the contract and agreement."

"District attorney? I thought you went down to Madison. I'm missing something. Just get here." Mia thankfully dropped the subject.

Sherrie, Mia, and I had been tight in college. Mia graciously accepted how much closer Sherrie and I had become since Sherrie moved in with me two years ago. Mia never questioned the friendship the three of us had. She understood that she misses out on some things.

"I'm almost there. Just stall a little bit more. I don't know, make up some crap about moving cars or fire safety shit. Tap my mom for help, she is good with this kinda stuff. I have to pick up someone. I'll be quick."

"Your mom. Awesome idea. Where is she? I forgot how when you get rolling, you get the rest of us of kick it up a notch. The town needs you here." Mia yelled at me and before the line went dead I heard her shout, "Katie Lyn!"

Five days ago, after the second time Ben Butler showed up on my phone, I replied, "Yes." A minute later, an address appeared. A minute later, "Saturday?" I confirmed yes without a time. The breadcrumbs were there, and so would be Chuck if I needed him. Not sure if it was smart to go alone.

CHAPTER TWENTY-SEVEN

The week of the funeral.

Everybody needs a Chuck in their life. No questions asked and someone who just does what you need without explanation.

Chuck was former military and current private security tech guy for some undisclosed company out of Texas. Or least that was what he told people. There may have been more physical security in undisclosed foreign lands than there is cyber-tech security. His mother chose to believe in the latter, and others knew not to ask questions. He was in his early thirties, had his own house and no known girlfriend but not to say he didn't have one.

He was also the older brother to my ex-boyfriend Aaron, the one before Pete. I sometimes forgot that little fact because my friendship with Chuck was independent from his brother. The friendship may have been one-sided as he was always helping me out of a jam. I wasn't sure what I brought to the table for him.

Pete died on a Thursday. His family and I planned the service for the following Thursday. The Tuesday before the service, I sent Chuck a message.

Can you watch the house, Pete's house, and his parents' house during the service.

There was no need to put a question mark on it. He would simply get it done even if he was at one those undisclosed locations he disappeared to for months at a time.

Since my accident, I had felt as if someone was watching. The mysterious person who got into the house while I was sleeping and other strange sightings. It was probably just everyone in town talking about the fire at the hardware store and all the gossip flying around and curious people pointing at me.

During the receiving line at funeral, Chuck talked to Pete's brothers briefly and then moved forward to me. He gave me a hug and just held me until I was ready to let go. He didn't say anything. Despite Chuck being at the church service, I knew our houses were being watched. He was one of the few people in line that didn't set their grief on me.

Seeing him broke the continuous heat wave of people crushing me with their support and the constant petting of my arms.

I looked to the rear of church where I had previously seen the familiar yet unknown man. I'd hope to point him out to Chuck, but the man was gone. This man never came forward to talk to me or Pete's family, or if he did, I was too lost in the moment at standing next to Pete's coffin to notice a lot of things.

During my drive to Madison on that Saturday, I told Chuck where I was going and just to track me. More questions came with that request but I didn't give him any more than that.

CHAPTER TWENTY-EIGHT

Days after the unthinkable happened.

Pete had been gone such a short time that I was still counting the distance in hours. My mom and dad were at the house. Work did not expect me for a few days, maybe a week. I didn't really remember the conversation. Tomorrow, I would meet with Peggy and Don to plan the funeral.

Sitting felt wrong now. All I did at the hospital was sit. The walls of the house were closing in on me. I wasn't sure of the time of day. Spring mist, rain, and gloom covered the weather and my mood.

I came out of my room with running clothes on with no intention of running, only running away for a while.

Sherrie was coming out of the bathroom and didn't hide her surprised look at me moving around. "Parents taking you somewhere?" she asked.

"Nope, just me."

I never run with anyone so she knew this was an escape. "Wait a sec." She left me in the hallway for a long minute. "Not sure how long you will be gone, but it might start raining. You can tie it around your waist if you're too warm."

We walked downstairs together and heard my mom talking to someone on the porch. "— appreciate the offer of the meal, but you have to understand multiple meals have been sent over. By the time we get to this, it will be past its prime. Now we understand you wanting to provide your support, but we are just overwhelmed with casseroles, potato dishes, and the like."

The lady's response was muffled, and my mom responded, "As I said, we have no room in the refrigerator, and the beef stew is already on the stove top. I will tell Claudia about the meal, but we cannot accept it. You may go to Mr. and Mrs. Morris's house and offer it to them, but I have a feeling they may be overloaded with people dropping things off. Yes, it is generous offer, and we don't want it to go to waste. Now, I don't want you get wet and the rain may be starting, so again thank you for the offer and condolences. Have a nice afternoon." My mom had one foot inside the living room as she spoke the last words.

"Now who was that?" Sherrie asked.

"Mrs. Bregg," my mom said.

"That was her this whole time?" Sherrie said.

"You don't have to do all the cooking. Maybe we should take a dish or two?" I said.

My mom laughed. "I am not taking anything from Mrs. Bregg. Craig, her son, a guy I had a crush on my senior year of high school, did not ask me to the senior prom. Wasted months flirting with him. He took my friend instead, and at the after party, he hit on me. If she can't raise a decent son, we don't need to take her food. I don't care if several decades have passed. She can take her funeral potatoes and give them to her precious son."

"Amen," Sherrie said.

"You going for a run?" my mom asked.

"Just a walk." I watched my mom hold her smile, and her eyes moved as if she was reading a menu above a counter at a restaurant. "Ok, if you want company, even silent company, I can go with you."

"I'm good. While I'm gone, you and Sherrie can finish that conversation she was miming behind me."

"Head out the back door and cross Jorge's yard so you don't have to walk past Mrs. Bregg."

My dad met me in the kitchen and held open the back door. When I turned right, he rotated me left. I walked and walked and walked.

I am a lone runner. Running groups are not my thing. I don't want to worry about having the breath to chitchat or keeping pace with others. I run to lose myself in the music, podcasts, exhaustion, and inner strength.

Today, I was just lost. I stopped walking when I realized I was thirsty. It took me forty seconds to figure out where I was along the river. I would always end my runs on the same spot and walk the last few blocks back home. Sometimes, Pete would track my runs and meet with a drink, and we would walk back together.

Today, there was no Pete.

Tomorrow, there will be no Pete.

I cut through some tall grass, taking a shortcut to the road to find a gas station or something that would sell me some water. Someone was running behind and made the same unconventional route as I did. The face was unfamiliar, and he seemed to be coming straight for me but turned north and kept an even pace running up the incline.

Relief rushed out of me, not because of fear of being attacked but more condolences and grief was what I was distancing myself from. I watched the man run when I heard a a vehicle come to a stop on the gravel shoulder behind me.

Happily—a word I haven't used much lately—I opened the truck door and plopped down only to wrestle with seat belt and my coat. "I know you are having a rough time lately, but have you lost all your coordination too?" my dad asked.

"It's just Sherrie's coat that wrapped around me is blocking the seat belt clip." I gave the windbreaker a tug, and my hand slipped and went flying into my forehead. The coat ripped and something dropped from the pocket. When I went down to pick up the item, I hit my head on the dashboard.

"Oh, C, not only did you lose the battle, I think you lost the war." My dad laughed. "There are probably napkins in the glove box. You might want to look at your forehead. You hit one of your scabs."

"Of course I did." I couldn't help but laugh at myself too. I held in my hand Sherrie's AirTag luggage tracker. "So this is why I was let out of the house on my own. Sherrie told you and mom that you could track my movements. Am I that lost?"

"It was out of love and you have been a little . . . C, first can you wipe your forehead." My dad waited as I found some napkins to dab my scabs. "I didn't follow you the whole time. As you can see, you are in the middle of nowhere. Do you even know how long you have been walking? You don't need to answer. I was just checking if you wanted water, a ride, or just more space?"

"All three I guess." I know now that was not any type of answer. My dad just kept driving down the country road.

"I wasn't sure what the best option was so I bought a little bit of everything. Grab whatever you like from the bag on the floor."

I had my pick of water, a six-pack of beer, and what brought tears to my eyes—chocolate Yoo-hoo. "You're the best."

I twisted the cap, turned around, and looked down the road.

"You drop something? Do I need to go back?" my dad asked.

"There was this guy running and now . . ."

"Shouldn't you wait until after the funeral, honey?"

A sad groan escaped me. "Oh, dad."

"I thought you and Sherrie were all about the inappropriate joke at the right time to lighten the mood. And before you say something, remember how mad your mother was at Nana's funeral because you were laughing."

"The joke was fine. Sherrie would be proud. It is just weird that he disappeared. I hardly knew he was behind me, and now he's gone. Not too many runners out here. More bikers this far down the path. Why cut up from the river just to head back down?"

"Do you think he was runner or a creep? Should we call police and just have them watch the area?"

My dad let me make the judgment call. "He looked and ran like a runner, but it's odd as to where he came from and went to. It's fine. I guess."

"While you were running, Don stopped over. He didn't say you need to call him or anything but just letting you know. He chatted with your mom and for a bit. I do think he wanted to talk to you."

CHAPTER TWENTY—NINE

In the hospital room.

I could hear Sherrie on phone.

"I don't know too much. Someone was talking, and then she collapsed."

. . .

"Her mom, Katie Lyn, is trying to get information, but doing it over the phone is not easy."

. . .

"Bump on the head. Don't know how long she was out."

. . .

"Also something about dehydration or food poisoning."

. . .

"I don't know what he knows?"

. . .

"I don't know when she will be able to talk."

. . .

"What do you mean the last number dialed?"

. . .

"You think whoever was in the house called and now threatened her?"

. . .

"I'll see what I can figure out. Have you seen anything?"

. . .

"Thanks for asking. I am good. I will keep you updated."

CHAPTER THIRTY

STILL THE MORNING AFTER I GOT ANOTHER MESSAGE "BEN BUTLER."

I was sure it a message from Pete or about Pete.

I thought.

I guessed.

I hoped.

Ben and Jerry's Cherry Garcia was his favorite ice cream. On the rare night he had nothing going on and I was working, his favorite thing to do was to watch a game, any game, on TV with his buddy "Ben."

Leroy Butler was one, not the only one, of his favorite Green Bay Packer players. He always told students who were struggling about Leroy Butler. As a child, Butler spent time in leg braces and a wheelchair before becoming a Hall of Fame defensive player in the NFL. The next part only makes sense if you understand football or sports in general: to push his point more about overcoming struggles as a defensive player, Butler creates this ongoing thirty-year tradition, the Lambeau Leap, most offensive players strive to be a part of.

Pete was telling me this was my time. Push past what I had lost and make the leap and maybe land with ice cream in hand.

CHAPTER THIRTY-ONE

PETE IS STILL IN THE HOSPITAL.

Sherrie had gotten a call from Jim at Draw Bar asking if she wanted to pick up hours bartending. Pete stated working there after he left Aaron's bar. She declined, and he asked her to come in to talk about it. He was rather pushy with his nonstop texting telling her to come in. He even suggested bringing me so I could help convince her to take the job to cover Pete's shifts and of course buy me a beer when I needed a break from the hospital.

I sent a text thanking him for the offer of a beer and said I would send Marcus. Jim responded so fast I thought he was standing behind me watching me type. He readily turned away the idea of Marcus and asked for me to come in. Something about the asking and not an offer of his "This is how I feel so I must tell someone closer to Pete how I feel" made me want to go see Jim.

I almost didn't go the next day when I got a text saying he was at the bar getting deliveries and I could use the back door if the front door wasn't open. I half wondered if he was going to tell me Pete was fired for missing his shifts.

That thought wasn't completely far off from what happened.

I walked around the truck parked in the alley and slid past some cases of frozen mozzarella sticks. Jim was on the phone yelling at someone about their start time that day. He gave me a one-arm hug and held up his index finger, telling me to give him a minute while he wrapped up the call.

I took a seat at the bar and listened as another truck backed down the alley. The beeping noise from the truck drowned out a portion of the phone call. Finally, Jim yelled into the phone, "Fine eleven thirty, but a minute later and you're fired."

He turned to me. "I'm glad you came in. No one ever guesses sometimes before a bar even opens, it can be nuts. Can I get you something? Listen, I wanted you here because . . ." Jim caught his breath and a piece of sanity before he spoke again, "How is he doing? Any changes?"

"Thanks for asking. No real change. He is mostly out of it. His temperature is high and . . ." I took a long, deep breath and paused. I had repeated this information so much.

In the last few days, Sherrie had taken over sending out the mass text updates. Sometimes talking about it could be therapeutic and other times overwhelming.

"You don't need to say anything. I really wanted you here to get the stuff out of Pete's locker." Jim put his elbows on the bar and leaned in, barely talking above a whisper. It was hard to hear him over the two deliver guys yelling at each other. "I didn't want to text you or have it on my phone or Pete's. The logical thing was trying to get Sherrie to bring you in here. I don't care what he does when he is not working, but gotta keep this place clean. Don't know what's gonna happen if the police dig deep. Would've taken care of it myself, but . . . I'm cool but you never . . ."

We heard a keg drop from an unknown height and hit the cement floor with a thud that made me not want to look down the hallway.

"Shit!" The vein on Jim's forehead was about to pop.

"Go take care of it," I said.

He scooted around the bar yelling, "Give Pete my best." More obscenities trailed out of Jim as he headed for the back door.

I dropped off the barstool and walked behind the bar. There were four small homemade plywood boxes with locks on them. Several years ago, a female employee had complained about no break room and no secure place to store her stuff while she worked. Jim would have fired her on the spot if he wasn't so scared of her suing him for something.

Sherrie and I would store the our coats while we barhopped in town while waiting for Pete to close the bar. The lock was a five-digit code issued by Jim. I couldn't help wonder why Jim needed me to clear Pete's box; what could he have in there?

This was one of bigger surprises in my life and that included my engagement, being gifted a house, losing someone I truly loved, becoming a widow and mother all within a year.

I put in the five-digit code, popped the lock off. Inside was just a plastic grocery bag. I didn't know the limit on the number of times someone can be gobsmacked in a week, but I was hitting my limit. The white plastic bag held four wads of cash-rolled up, bound with rubber bands, of various denominations and a well-used brown paper lunch bag with several plastic bags full of weed. Oh, and a switchblade.

If that wasn't enough, I got a text from EG.

> Everything in the house is good.
> Coming to see you. Wait on more
> renovations.

How could everything be good, I wondered.

CHAPTER THIRTY-TWO

Every day Pete was in the hospital I learned something about humanity.

The first few nights, I had slept at the hospital. The vinyl recliner chair provided more comfort than one would think being found in a hospital room yet it was no bed with Pete spooning me.

I couldn't read Peggy if she thought it only a Morris family responsibility and/or being engaged was sufficient entry into the family. Each morning, she and Don would arrive at seven thirty and remain there all day.

I didn't back down for the first three nights, and then I finally relented and went home for a night. Marcus's nervous energy was too much anytime he was in the room. Asking the same questions, trying to find a reason Pete was not getting better.

The thought of having him spending the overnight hours in the hospital would have pushed the nurses to their limit and might have actually gotten his visitation hours restricted. Don't know if that was a thing or not in a hospital, but something had to give.

Peggy and Don listened carefully each time a nurse or doctor came in. The day shift nurse, Mary, learned by the morning of day two and her sixth update with us just to let Peggy ask her questions. All the questions resulted in the same answers. I followed Mary out of the room the second morning on the premise of getting more coffee.

I stood outside the door and leaned against the wall. I was claustrophobic from the machines beeping, Peggy's questions, Don's Googling every medical term, and even the sunlight pushing down on us.

"Hon, you gotta have patience," Mary said.

"I know it will take time for him to get better."

"That's not what I'm talking about. Her questions. I learned a long time ago not to take it personally. Some relatives are overwhelmed with the information. Some have no comprehension of the medicine. Some believe their questions will be the cure. Peggy, I have known since our kids were in grade school. Like me, she is the mother of three kids and she, like me, learned early to ask questions, sometimes the same one, just to see if you get the same answer. It's called parenting. It doesn't stop. Not even when your kids leave the house. You will understand it one day."

The next day, my vision of Marcus being asked to leave the hospital almost came to fruition when I walked in at six, and he was having words with the night nurse, Cheryl.

"Sir, at this hour, no one gets past security without signing in, and most importantly, no one gets past my desk. I got eyes on everything on my wing. If someone entered Mr. Morris's room, it was a hospital employee. If you want to remain on the list of approved visitors, I suggest we both forget this conversation ever happened." Cheryl left Marcus standing outside Pete's room and returned to her workstation in the center of the wing.

I tried handing Marcus a coffee, but he waved me off before heading to the bank of elevators. I dropped the white paper bags off at the nurses station.

"Did he call us *girls*?" Cheryl said.

"Does it matter?" I asked. "Everything is still warm."

On my way in, I'd stopped at Peach's that morning for breakfast. They didn't open til six thirty, but Ellie, our dear friend, was part of the morning opening crew. She opened the door for me and collected twenty-six dollars worth of pastries and two coffees. As I was leaving, Grumpy Freddie came running from the kitchen and tossed two more bags at me. "Those girls on the blue wing took real good care of my mother."

Cheryl reached for the hand sanitizer and then the bag. She hesitated before she spoke, "You seem like good folk. So I am telling you this and will not ever repeat this for anyone. It's not the first time someone tried to serve court papers here in a hospital, but I won't let it happen on my watch. Serving papers to good folk ain't happening while someone is recovering. Law or no law, not on my watch."

"Pete's awake?" I asked. Tears flooded my eyes. Pete had been in and out consciousness since the explosion. "Is he upset? Did the guy talk to him?"

"There's been no change. Like I said. No one gets in a room without me knowing it. The man never entered the room. Mr. Morris slept through all of it, and nothing affected him. Miss, I think the guy was looking for you. From what I heard, the papers could be for either one one you."

"If Freddie can't call you 'girls,' please don't call me miss. It's Claudia." I felt spicy that morning

and knew it had to be a good day. Prayed for it to
be a good day, and it did not disappoint.

CHAPTER THIRTY-THREE

I THINK THE SECOND EVENING OR JUST A LOT OF HOURS
AFTER PETE WAS ADMITTED TO HOSPITAL.

"Please stop laughing," Sherrie asked of Jenna. They were sitting in the waiting area outside the bank of elevators that separated three different wings of the hospital.

"I still have my winter weight on me. Been driving more than usual this spring. Anxious to get back on my bike since I've been eating like I am still biking a hundred miles a week. These sweats are comfy."

They stopped laughing, and without speaking, I knew the question they were going to ask.

"Nothing has changed. They're keeping him sedated until they have a full understanding of what is keeping his temperature so high. Still monitoring his heart and lungs. He has a weak heart. He inhaled a lot of smoke. They can handle the burns here without sending him to a burn unit. Right wrist broken and left ankle is sprained, or is it the other way around. Some broken ribs."

"That still sucks," Sherrie said mirroring my inner thoughts. "Not sure how long you will be here, so I grabbed you some clean comfy clothes, a toothbrush, and stuff."

"I appreciate it." I turned to Jenna. "Have you heard anything at work? When Pete was briefly awake, he was not making too much sense."

Jenna worked for a judge at the courthouse, and she seemed to know everyone that worked in the River Bend Justice Center. "I haven't seen the police report. Don't know if it's officially been filed, but from what I gather, piecing it together; remember this is only snippets. Not sure of fact or opinion."

I raised my open hand to stop her preface. "I get it. This is not a courtroom. No one is under oath. We are not going to quote you or even repeat one word. Just give me some idea of why we are sitting here."

She pulled out a memo pad like she was a secretary from the '70s. "Several customers heard shouting. Most agree it was Pete and Phil. Don't know if Patty was involved from the start or if she tried to break up the agreement. The stories are too vague to know what the argument was about."

Jenna was slow and methodical as she spoke. Each line became etched in my memory. My hands folded like I was praying, but I just squeezing them to redirect my heartache and keep my tears from falling. *Did Pete set the fire?* The police had been here looking for that exact answer, and no could give it to them.

Jenna continued, "Patty was seen running around the store. Unsure if it was before or after Pete left. He was seen leaving the hardware store through the rear door. It was noted that is odd behavior since your Jeep was parked out front.

"Now order of events really vary depending on who is telling the story. Pete ran back in or Phil ran out after Pete or Pete chased Phil. Then there was the explosion. Pete went in and out of the building several times. He was pulling customers out of the store. They think at one point, he either got trapped by the smoke and flames or something fell and hit his head, and that's why the firefighters had to lift him out.

"The police do know the last number he dialed on his cell was Phil's, so it is suggested that Pete may have gone there to confront him about your accident."

"I gave them access to his phone records," I said.

The three of us just looked at each other.

Sherrie broke the silence, "There is a lot more on the paper. Don't hold back."

"Most of it is repetitive or conjuncture. Making sure I didn't miss anything I wrote down. If anything new is discovered, I will let you know."

I sat back in the stiff waiting room chair. Across from me, Jenna and Sherrie were on a small sofa. Between me and them was a coffee table with a half-done puzzle. I couldn't help think I wish I had the mindless energy to fixate on wild horses running through a stream. I did have my own puzzle to figure out, however it might have been more than five-hundred perfectly cut pieces.

The fog of information Jenna shared with us lifted when I looked at Sherrie. It was my grandma's funeral all over again. Laughing when we shouldn't be. To be fair, Grandma would not be happy with laughing at any funeral much less hers but would want to know what we would be laughing at and may even enjoy a giggle when the time was right.

"What are you wearing?" I asked.

"Well." Sherrie waited for us to drop the topic, but she knew she had to explain. "I showered and was half-dressed when I had the idea to bring stuff for you. I was in your room looking for clothes when I heard someone in the yard. I couldn't see anything from your window so I went back to my room and then to yours again. It was a weird noise."

She stopped talking. Jenna and I assumed for dramatic effect, then it hit me. The bones that were buried, discovered, and reburied by someone who was in the house while I there!

I believed Sherrie altered the story to leave out everything she was afraid of and that included the buried bones coming alive and rattling around.

Outside of Pete and Jorge, our circle of trust was just that small. Chuck was not even on that list. Jenna was someone we could trust with lots of stuff, but bones and reburied bones were a whole new level of trust. We didn't know if Jorge shared any of the details with her. Their relationship was new, and he understood it was not his story to share. It wasn't secret keeping when it was not your story.

Sherrie continued, "I ran downstairs, looked out the side window then the kitchen windows. Someone turned the corner, so I ran to the front bedroom and watched someone approach the screen door to the porch. The guy was wearing black and had a hood on. I don't know what I was thinking. People come over all the time, and I am not nervous." She started to laugh. "I was acting like a feral wolf."

"Is there such a thing?" I asked. "There is a feral cat and rabid dog or . . ."

Sherrie's feet rocked back and forth on the coffee table. "I don't know. Just saying I was freaked out wanting to scare away whoever was there. So I ran to the front door, swung it open, shouted something. It was at that time, the guy, actually a high school kid, was knocking on the porch screen looking directly at me. We both realized I only had on a bra and underwear."

Jenna and I fell into full-on laughter.

"The kid was saying Pete's name and something about a church. He had stopped talking once he—"

"Once he realized he was looking at half-naked girl," I choked out. "I haven't tried to scare away a lot of people lately, but I would probably make sure I was dressed."

She ignored me. " I really just wanted to see who it was. I had music playing so they knew someone was home. Couldn't figure out why they were walking around the house. When I heard Pete's name, I yelled for him to wait, not move, and ran up to grab some clothes. I threw on these sweets and my . . . blue . . ."

"HA!" I laughed. "You put on big blue. Your winter puffer jacket. Did you put up the hood?"

Sherrie nodded. "When I went back down, he was still there."

184

"Of course he was. You left the teenage boy stunned," Jenna said.

"He asked for Pete, and I said he wasn't here. The kid asked when and where he could find him. Pete owed him, and he had done everything. He was mad Pete wasn't at work yesterday or today. He kept saying Pete owes him. I asked him what he was owed money for, and he got a little squirrelly. He didn't want to say anything more, so I said unless he tells me, I'm telling Pete not to pay him.

"He went off on some rant, like a deal is a deal. He took care of what he needed to. At least give him some of what is owed so he could buy the prom tickets and money down for the tux or limo or something. He was rambling and wouldn't look at me."

I jumped in. "The kid couldn't look at you. Big blue puffer jacket was not hiding the images of you half-naked dancing in his head."

"He said he just needed some of it. He would do more work later when the weather was better. The kid was nearly in tears. He seemed sincere so I told him to wait, and I grabbed fifty bucks. He was unsatisfied. He said the tickets were eighty. At this point, I started to negotiate with how much he needed and what Pete really owed him. He wouldn't give me a figure on what Pete owed him for, besides saying yard work. The church was cleaned up, and no one needs their lawn cut right now. He said he cleared out all the dead stuff left from last fall from around the house but not much else he can do now. Like I said, he seemed sincere but twitchy.

"I ran back up and got seventy-five dollars."

"Who has that much cash these days?"Jenna asked.

"It's from my bartending days. My dad always carried twenty dollars cash with him. 'You just never know who is going to need an extra buck,' he would say. It always stuck with me. So I kept the singles when we were paid out for tips at the end of the night."

"So let me get this straight . . . you appear almost naked in front of this kid and come back with one-hundred twenty-five dollars in singles, and you're gorgeous. No wonder he can't look at you, he probably thinks you're a stripper." I paused a beat before I added, "Stripper or not, you are a better person than me. I don't know if I would have paid the kid anything. Pete's name is not an automatic password."

Jenna had two solid but conflicting points. "Who could make up a bullshit story like that? However, my only thing is that the entire town and probably county heard about the hardware store being blown up and Pete's unknown involvement and him being in the hospital . . ." Jenna's voice

186

trailed off. "Maybe thought he was home already from the hospital."

We sat there no longer laughing, only hearing the tick of an old wall clock beating away the seconds of this nightmare.

Finishing the story Sherrie mumbled, "So I threw on this sweatshirt, kept the comfortable sweats, and grabbed the bag of clothes for Claud and here I am."

CHAPTER THIRTY-FOUR

THE THIRD NIGHT, MAYBE THE FOURTH OR SIXTH NIGHT IN HOSPITAL JUST BEFORE DAWN I WOKE TO MY HAND BEING SQUEEZED. PETE WAS AWAKE.

Tears flowed down my dry cheeks and cracked lips. I had fallen asleep hunched over in a chair next to Pete's bed. With a ever so slight tug, he pulled me close. His voice was barely above a whisper.

"Mary," he said.

His eyes closed again, but he kept his hand on mine.

A short time later he said, "Patty."

If I didn't love this guy so much and knew how crazy he was for me, I would or should have been offended with his first two words being other women's names. I took into consideration Mary was the delightful daytime nurse who kept his pain medicine on task, and Patty was probably the last woman he had seen before the firemen carried him out.

His third word was more depressing. "Pills." Pete was out again.

Should I call the doctor or nurse in? Probably but I didn't want to share him with anyone. Not this morning. The mornings were our favorite time of day. I knew he was absolutely the one for me after a morning run. He told me he loved me one morning after I made him a frozen waffle. He proposed on the corner of Duke in the morning.

He had been in and out the previous day, but here it actually seemed he had been awake. The doctors had kept him sedated for a while for some reason or another, but we all hoped he would wake up now on his own. The fourth time he woke up, he was back to "Mary." I figured he needed more pain pills. I shouted for Mary. Cheryl, the night nurse, came in looking like I'd said I didn't like her cooking.

I was shaking and couldn't help smile as I said, "He's awake. I think he's heard everything because he is asking for Mary and pills. Pete squeezed my hand, and this time he said, "Not Mary."

"You need pain meds? Cheryl can do that. No, wait, I can push that button, and it will drip through the tubes, I think. Someone said something about that." I ran my fingers through his hair for the millionth time. His eyes were open this time, barely.

"I can do a lot of stuff, sir, but the lady is right. Name is Cheryl. I don't even answer to Ms. Nightingale. Pain button is just right here." Cheryl put the beige sticklike device in his right hand then adjusted some knobs on the machines next to his bed.

"Mary." Pete choked out again.

"Not with it, is he?" Cheryl said with a wink that I didn't know if it was meant to be humorous or stressing her observation of Pete's current mental capacity.

Pete never turned away from me. He managed a small smile and said, "Marry me."

"Already said I would."

"Now, marry me now." He squeezed my hand again and didn't let go. It was the most beautiful and saddest moment of my life. Something inside of him knew he wasn't going to make it, and yet he wanted me. I couldn't move, and I wasn't sure if I was even breathing. I wanted every second to count.

I didn't even hear the doctor come in. Pete never took his eyes away from me when the doctor poked him, adjusted tubes and IV stuff. He asked Pete basic questions of what's his name and what year it was. One would think you need a sense of humor or a little piece of humanity when working overnight in a hospital. This doctor did not appreciate the answers of "Claudia's wanna-be husband" and the year being "too many days not being married."

"Wow, I didn't know you are such a sap," I said.

"I am what I am. Now, marry me."

PART 2

CHAPTER THIRTY-FIVE

EG's Story.

Oh, the bones. It started this all. To be honest, Pete's weakened heart would've taken him out in a year or two. It was probably falling for Claudia that kept him going along as he had. The confrontation with Patty might have been my fault; however, no one is blameless in this story.

I would have told the story earlier, but we all agreed to never talk about it. It was one of those agreements that was just assumed. Not a nonverbal stare down, dramatic final parting words, or knowing glances across a room or city block. This was just common sense one was never to talk about something so . . . so . . . so . . . As a writer, I should have the words, but sometimes I just don't have the words. Also, partly because I never knew the body was in *my* basement.

It is amazing what people overlook or see only what you tell them to look at. I have a fabulous group of friends that travel together. We come from all over the country. No two of us are from the same state or have any family connection. We found each other at a writers conference although I am the only writer. Names are irrelevant. Not because I have to hide their identity, because they are innocent in all of this. I keep their names from you as not to give you more information to process.

We found each other three blocks from the hotel where I was a guest speaker. I wanted a moment away from the crowd as did the other ladies. We each had walked past the two bars directly across from our hotel.

I almost didn't attend the conference because of one of the gentlemen on the author panel was—there is no other word for him—an ass. Details are not important, but to give you an understanding of the man, I will tell you how he brought us together.

It's been done before so no points for originality, but the amount of information the process server unloaded on the man was epic. After the panel, each of us speakers stood in a corner of a room for the author meet and greet portion of the conference. This man, who wanted his own room because he expected such a large crowd, suddenly found himself with the shortest line. Not sure if it is ethical and or outside her line of duties, but not only did the process server—we call her Hiker A—hand him the divorce papers, she continued to lay it all out for him. She had agreed to wear a camera so the soon-to-be-divorced wife could watch it unfold.

Hiker A told him 90 percent of all the bank accounts have been cleared out, the children are with his soon-to-be ex, of course the dog is with her, the house is sold, and the closing date is in four days, and he shouldn't contest it as that is his only source of income, his publisher is aware the discrepancies in his fact-checking, both girlfriends are now aware of each other, and he needs to get checked for an STD.

From across the room, I didn't hear the conversation, but I saw the man turn white, wobble, and drop. The hotel worker—we'll call her Hiker R—so young and new she still had "trainee" under her name on her brass name badge. She had the steel calm to radio security for them to call for an ambulance but worried she would be sued for choking the man to death when she preformed CPR and accidentally spit her gum into his mouth effectually blocking her attempts to resuscitate the man.

The fourth one in our group—we'll call her Hiker L—was in town for a job interview she had decided to skip when she read a profile about the company in a national newspaper. She crashed the conference and had attended three of the breakout sessions. She was not there when the man dropped but didn't want to hang out with the paid attendees fearing she would get busted for not paying the entrance fee.

We stayed until the two a.m. bar time. Not only did we exchange our contact information, we booked an overnight stay at a mountain lodge an hour away from that hotel three weeks from when we met. Me, known as Hiker E. Just E, not EG, the Job Interviewee and the Process Server all had to fly back in, but we made it happen in a short time span. The three of us paid for the hotel worker. She was grateful and said that would be the last time she would accept our money. She got a second job to pay for annual trips. A second job while working in a hotel is not easy because the hours are erratic at best.

I tell you about the ladies because it is important to know they have no ties to River Bend or my personal life. We have our adventures and go back to our lives. They don't know my local friends or family personally or me theirs. So when I tell my sister or Claudia that I have a trip planned with the troop, they usually ask where and to suggest I have fun. People say it takes a village to raise a child. I think it takes a troop — or EARLs we like to call ourselves — to ground a person. Boy, did I need them now more than ever.

We don't attend each others' weddings or attend milestone birthday parties. We only meet up outside of our respective residences. It is all four of us or none of us. The trips have been as crazy as hiking across the Norway to the mundane of a rustic cabin in Indiana or a cheap flight somewhere for all of us to binge-watch *Downton Abbey*.

Again, I tell you all this nonsense so when I don't return with stunning photos or epic stories, it is not out of the ordinary. Also, when I say I am hiking with the troop, it is a great alibi. Like now when I am supposed to be with my troop, but I am with my husband, no one is any wiser.

CHAPTER THIRTY–SIX

STILL EG' STORY.

You read that last part correctly . . . husband. I was with my husband when I got Claudia's first texts about her having questions about the house, but when we were to finally connect, I was with my troop.

Pity is not my thing. Sympathy and well wishes are fine, needed, and occasionally wanted. I lived most of my life in River Bend as the widow. I mourned at his memorial, but I resented carrying that title. I had a whirlwind romance, quick marriage, and faster death so people projected the title of widow on me, which I didn't want, to weigh me down.

Why did I stay in River Bend as long as I had? I am not sure I know why. Maybe by the time I am done explaining this all, it might come to me.

However, the last few years, I spent more time at my place in Chicago and traveling than I did in River Bend.

It is a good house, not a great house. What was great was that I was able to buy my first home shortly after college graduation and have it paid off in under ten years. Is River Bend that affordable, my writing that profitable, or I just know how to handle financial stuff? Its a combination of all three.

It was easy saying good bye now to the house. It no longer felt as if it were mine. One of the highlights has been watching Claudia, the daughter I had but never expected to have or wanted. I was always meant to be the fun aunt. Claudia and her friend Sherrie made this town their home. I wasn't around much to watch Claudia and Pete together, but like everyone else, I knew they were right for each other.

I've been rambling on about people, I know, I know, I know—it's about the bones. I am getting to that. Writing this all out has me in a tailspin. When I write my fiction stories, I am short on hyperbole and let the actions tell the story. My editor is quick with the red pen and keeping the story on track. This is more of confessional or tell-all so let me be me.

When I returned Claudia's texts and she didn't respond in ten minutes, I guessed she was at work, so I called Pete since figuring any renovations being done to the house would involve him. Don't they know the only thing I could really tell them is where the manuals for the stove and microwave are located and the name of the handymen I hired to do anything in the house? I really wanted to cut and run from River Bend. Not necessarily from the girls but the town.

Pete answered quickly and was asking questions as if he were speaking Latin. My time and patience were short. I gifted Claudia the house, and it was for them to do with it what they want. I am not a landlord. My cell plan—no matter how good of phone plan you have while you are in the remote parts of the planet—either the reception is shitty or it does cost you more money. When he finally spit out, "There is a body buried under the tank," without having prior knowledge, I instantly knew what it meant.

Shock, disbelief, awe, anger, admiration, and the oh-shit factor to my engagement to this new entanglement, this where my editor usually knocks out of some of my word choices and forces me to choose, but I am letting them all in. All those emotions washed over me, and I was told I muttered "Patty" before I dropped. My head hit the table before it bounced on the floor.

No one was lying when my sister, Katie Lyn, called and spoke to the husband of someone in our troop. It's just no one realized it was my husband.

CHAPTER THIRTY-SEVEN

EG's Story Continues

I met Duncan when he was a grad student at Jameson College. I had graduated from a college in Minneapolis with decent success as a writer. For most writers, that means an extra helping of ramen. For me, it meant I had a steady job writing under a pen name for a women's magazine and dumb luck finding an agent and selling my first book. The lack of success with my second book put me back on the ramen diet, but at least I was eating it in my own kitchen, even if that kitchen didn't have a table. I reused plastic cutlery I'd collected from fast food joints, not as part of recycling, but as the only utensils I had.

The move back to River Bend after having lived in the city during college was pretty easy and petty. I knew my writing earning would cap out sooner than later. Every creative writing and journalism professor pounds that into your head. At least the good ones did. I had money in the bank leaving college. Not many students leave ahead of the game.

It had been a year since giving birth to Claudia and giving her to my sister and her husband to raise as their own. I wanted something stable, and I knew living in the cities would have me out at night, skipping out on my writing time, and giving up on my writing career too soon. It was also awesome coming back as a single female, purchasing my own home, and showing off to those from my high school days that did not think much of me.

Duncan was an international student from Scotland. He had the charming accent with a smile and dimples reserved for a teen heart throb boy-band member. He gave me a gift the day before my birthday, just so I would know he knew it was my birthday and no one had to remind him. He'd ask questions about my childhood in River Bend, my dreams, my writing.

The whirlwind romance masked a lot of things. What I thought was a curious mind and longing for family was really insecurity. The other red flag I missed was his lack of sense of humor. Especially being able to laugh at himself.

The quiet bombshell dropped on our relationship when a professor at Jameson College asked about our collaborative writing technique. I had been a guest speaker the previous semester in that creative writing class. This year she was hoping I could talk to this class about benefits of group and team workshopping story ideas.

The professor saw the confused look on my face. "Sorry, I just assumed you work together. Writers in the same house. How could you not talk about your work? The mini series you started last month in the magazine mirrored so much with Duncan's stories he has been putting out for the weekly short story assignment. Change out your idea of your heroine hitching hiking across fifty states to train travel across the UK, and your stories line up.

This professor may have known how to write but not how the publishing company worked or at least how it worked back in my magazine days. I had submitted the complete series six months ago. So that meant all the writing and editing had been done long before Duncan was part of my life.

I left the professor and my grocery cart in the aisle and did what I knew to do in River Bend. I walked and walked and walked and did some thinking. Like most writers, I am very protective of my work. Themes, plots, and the usual Hollywood endings overlap from book to book and movie to movie. It is natural as there are only so many ways a story can go. The Lion King runs the theme of Hamlet just to give you idea. Was the story stolen from Shakespeare? Of course not, but it demonstrates how some stories are created and built upon the works of others.

Every writer struggles. I once saw an interview with the great song writer David Foster. You know the guy with endless Grammy awards and nominations. The man's career is legendary. He has written and produced song for artists from every genre and has a roomful of trophies to prove how talented he is. Yet he said he doubts himself at least two or three days a week. Not three times a week, three whole DAYS a week. Only one day a week he may think he is a genius, and the other days are full of doubt. It is the one great day of writing that blocks away the doubt.

What do we do when we doubt our writing? That depends on the writer. Sorry I don't have the magical answer for you. You might be disappointed you if you are hoping for a writing career and seeking me for guidance. I just know what I do. If I am stuck on a storyline, I first walk away from the computer. Literally walk away and go for a walk to clear my head. Most times, I don't even think about the story. When I return to my computer, I erase the last three chapters. Although that is painful to do, as any words typed out are precious words on a page, I erase three chapters, not even rereading them before I do it. I wrote myself into a hole, and this is the best way out. Sometimes, I toss in another walk before I write.

That is a long way of saying I never look to someone else's writing while I am in the middle of a project. I don't want their thoughts meandering into MY storyline. So to hear someone, and someone close to me, has been using my stories as their own, it floored me. I am not a muse or storyboard for someone else.

I am not even sure when or where I was on my walk when I had the light bulb moment. I just started running. Running can you believe that? Me, running. I was dressed for a quick trip to the grocery store, not a walk, much less a run. Are we sure what the professor said was true? I had two blisters forming within three minutes of running.

Let me take you back and talk about when we first met. Duncan had asked me to critique his work. I was hesitant to do it because I am honest when talking about my craft. It's hard to flirt with someone while telling them their work sucks, or even if it doesn't suck, could they handle even the slightest suggestion? I found his initial writing on point with telling a story but to dig deeper with the characters. He took the feedback well and asked me on a date.

Since then I'd kept asking to see more work, and he had always declined. He was looking to date me and not for a mentor. He wanted to keep work separate. During my walk after speaking with the professor, I remembered an incident from earlier. He still had his living arrangements on campus for international students, but it was not unusual for him to come over and wait for me to get home. I had come in through the porch door and found him coming down the stairs with his backpack.

I hadn't expected him until later. "What nice surprise, but I wasn't expecting you until later. I need about thirty minutes to get some writing done, but we can do an early dinner and go see that movie."

"Oh, I don't think I can do any of that. I got some stuff I need to do for a project. The company

I sent some of freelance articles reached out and wanted more samples of my writing. That's why I am here. I can't find a folder with the material I have been working on. Thought maybe I left in your office, that's why I'm here. Maybe one of my mates snagged it by mistake. We'll figure out our plans later. Want to get my work done so I can happily focus on you and not be thinking of what I need to do."

"Do you need help looking? I have a good eye for things," I said.

"I know you do, babe." He kissed my cheek and walked out the front door.

"Let know me if you need me to turn your place over," I yelled, not sure if he heard me, and he shuffled back to campus.

I went up upstairs, dropped my bag on the floor and did a cursory look around. No notebook or folder of his caught me eye, but if he had looked and hadn't found it, it must not be there. I sat at my desk and pounded out thirty minutes of good writing that translated to two hours of actual time. Something was bothering me, and I couldn't figure it out. I thought it was maybe the plotline I was working on. When I got thirty minutes of quality writing, that shouldn't be what was bothering me.

Then it dawned on me. He had heard from someone that wanted more samples of his writing. That was great news. As writers, especially ones just starting out, we get such little good news or positive feedback that you want to shout from the top of the mountaintop. Not so everyone can hear because we know it is just a request, but yelling it from the top of your lungs makes it more real and validating as an author.

Not everyone processes the information the same way as I do. It just bummed me out that he didn't want to share the good news with me. Not even for a minute to rehash the phone call. I assumed it was a phone call, maybe it was a letter. This was a time before everything was done via email and texting.

He called later that evening and canceled our plans so he could get his writing done. We had been dating for six months at that point. Disappointed but I understood the need to write especially when someone is interested in your work.

I didn't hear from him for three days. He showed up at my house wearing a semi-pressed shirt carrying a bouquet of flowers. He only had one long-sleeve button-down shirt with him. He had been living out of two suitcases of clothes.

My mood was rather pouty because of the three-day hiatus from me, but the dopey grin and effort to look nice cracked me up. He came in and immediately starting talking. He talked nonstop for fifteen minutes about his writing, us, school, his mom, our future, his writing again. He only stopped when I laughed. He expression changed from a jubilant kid-like mania to sunken defeat. "I am not laughing at you, only with you. Just caught up in all your glee. Do you need something to drink?"

"Of course, babe." His smiled returned. "Wait, I brought something. I am such a mess. Let me get my head on right and do this proper."

He grabbed his bag and went into the kitchen leaving me with instructions to stay on the sofa. He returned two minutes later sans any beverage.

"That was a lot of time in the kitchen to return empty-handed."

"It is, isn't it. I realized with all my rambling there is an order to some things. So, as I was saying before, you and me . . ."

There was a whole lot more said. Most of it sweet like what everyone hopes to hear from their partner and some more nervous ramblings. Some I don't want to share because it is private and I want to believe in love without judgment from others. He ended up on one knee in front of me holding a ring box asking, "Will you marry me?"

A instant yes yelped from my body. He pulled me forward, kissed me, and abruptly left me on the sofa. He ran back into the kitchen returning with a bottle of champagne. We toasted our happiness. I called my sister, and she was happy and a little surprised as most people were when I told them but still happy for me.

He didn't want to call his mom as it was a six-hour time difference. Her health was poor, and the best chance of her being fully aware of things was typically midmorning. When Duncan was five, his father had died in a factory accident, and he was estranged from his brother who'd left home at seventeen and he had only seen twice in the ten years since he left.

He best mate, Craig, knew already as he had called him asking if Americans expect something different than back home for a proposal. He was worried about the size of the ring. It had been his grandmother's. I told him I loved the sentimental value of the ring. The one emerald stone next to the small diamond made it gorgeous.

Two days later, he trotted over with a suitcase and a half of belongings. He still kept his room on campus as his writing area. It was paid in full for two years as part of the scholarship program he had been awarded.

We held the ceremony three months later at the courthouse with my sister and his roommate from Poland as our witnesses. We had planned to do it sooner but had to wait for his mother's caregiver to send over some legal documents he needed.

Living together was an easy adjustment. We both needed our own areas when writing. He didn't bring really any personal items that I had to negotiate space for in my house. His only thing he insisted on, I couldn't really say no to, was his alarm clock with the extra big numbers so he could see the time without his contacts. The clock illuminated the room like a Taco Bell sign at bar time.

Our one fight was when he disappeared again for three days writing. I didn't mind that he needed the space or time, but a phone call was what I needed. I had come home, and he was in the upstairs bathroom. He jumped about ten feet when he walked into the office and saw me at my desk. "Thought you are coordinating the high school book club today. I was writing here for once at our home, but that is messed up now."

"Stay and write. I'm just dropping off stuff and meeting Kathleen for drinks."

"No, really I just wanted one of your research books so I'm good now. I'm going to write at my space."

He left the house and left me in a sour mood. At least he didn't tear apart the office looking for the book he needed. I didn't want to suggest that any of my research books should be used with caution as the terminology greatly differs between the States and Britain. It is something I learned the hard way when setting a story in Canada. My editor has not stop complaining about the research she had to do to correct my mistakes, and it's been two years and three books later.

Several hours later, I returned from meeting Kathleen at the bar, having had more drinks than I intended. I fell asleep on the sofa and awoke to a phone call. It was all so strange. The man had an accent same as Duncan, but the man was asking for Robert. I told him he had the wrong number and hung up. The man called back repeating himself. I laughed at the man not understanding a drunk American accent accepting my theory he had the wrong number. Finally in my sleepy drunk state, I told him would have someone call him back.

The lesson here is, listen when people speak.

Duncan showed up three days later smiling, giddy, and ready to kick back and relax. He said the last three days he had gotten some of his best writing done. He had faxed the samples of his work to a British literary agency, and they had already responded with positive feedback and want him to write for a British children's magazine.

He had brought over a bottle of champagne to celebrate. We toasted his success, and I said I would make one of his favorite dinners that night. He wanted to keep the celebration going all afternoon, but I said I had to write and prep for my talk at the high school. Without a trace of modesty, I added he would know that if he had bothered to call his wife anytime in the last seventy-two hours. He didn't understand why we just couldn't celebrate his success and that everything revolved around my schedule.

A lot of words were exchanged mostly about understanding what someone needs like support for the good and bad, and what it means to be married. Our voices were raised and tears were shed. We retreated to separate corners of the house. I had gone to my favorite spot on the porch, and he was somewhere, I didn't care where as long as he did not follow me out to the porch. I sat and stewed for a bit but still made him chicken paprikash. At some point, he had left only to return with flowers, an alarm clock for his work area, and my favorite wine.

The next seven days, he was gone twelve to fourteen hours a day, but he would call me every fours hours. He told me he had bought the alarm clock not because he needed a reminder to call me but to break his concentration. I totally understood what he meant. I once burnt a frozen pizza so badly my neighbors called the fire department because of the smoke they smelled from their driveway. I was so engrossed in my writing upstairs I didn't sense the air was full of burnt pizza and that annoying but soft beeping was my kitchen smoke detector. It was quite a commotion on the street, but I laughed it off as it was some of the best writing I had done all week.

The following week he spent going to class, cleaning, and taking care of everything around the house I was ignoring because I was on a deadline. Thursday night, he had made shepherd's pie and said the last three weeks have been the best three weeks of his life. Including our fight, adding he learned what I needed and how he could be a better husband. Not having a father figure in his life and never seeing his mother with a decent man, he only knew how to take care of himself.

Sometimes, you know when you picked a good guy.

The next night, we walked along the river debating the merits of a pen name for his series he had been commissioned to write. I thought if it was such a wide publication like a magazine, he has to use his name. I asked what his agent suggested, and he said he was dealing direct with the magazine and hoped to find an agent for the book series he is working on. He didn't want his name to be tied to children's fiction. He wanted to be taken as a serious writer.

We stood by the Mississippi River skipping rocks, swatting away mosquitoes, finding the remaining orange and red leaves that had fallen from the maple trees, and tossing out pen names. Everything from the mundane John Moore, sounding both English and American, a pretentious name George Earl the Third, or something mysterious like only using a first initial D. Smith. It was one of the moments of just the two of us that I hoped to last forever.

The last few weeks had been wonderful, but underneath Duncan's happy facade something was bothering him. I chalked it up to being nervous before receiving his writing contract and the stress of school. He still had to perform at an above-average GPA for the scholarship.

The free tuition for his master's program was incredible. I had never thought for him to pay any of the mortgage or house bills. It was just something I took care of without much thought. It was with great pride I could do all this on my own in my mid-twenties. Was it generosity or selfishness that I didn't want help from anyone including my new husband?

When we walked home after the sun set across the Mississippi, we heard the phone ringing but neither one of us rushed inside to get it. We stood on the porch kissing, and the phone rang again. We didn't break our embrace but strangely waited for the ringing to stop. "Hey, maybe you should call yourself Robert Morgan. Keep your surname but change it to Robert, you know keeping it semi-mysterious, the big man of young adult horror thriller books."

"No thanks," Duncan said and walked into the house, leaving me without someone to hug.

"That was a sharp response from someone who ten minutes ago was considering Theo Morton Cheshire." I laughed.

"Why would you even suggest that name?" He stood with his hands on his hips like a teacher wanting to know what kid threw the spitball at their neck. I was speechless and motionless standing just inside the living room. It was a standoff until I realized my thoughtlessness and said, "I was thinking you have only called your brother Bobby. I only thought of it because of the ringing phone. A couple of weeks ago, when you were gone for those days, someone called asking for Robert and for Robert to call Duncan or was it a Robert calling for a Duncan. It was a strange, weird phone call."

"You never thought to tell me me someone called for me?" Duncan said.

"I was drunk and asleep. Barely remember the conversation. I just thought it was a wrong number. Forgotten about it until we heard the phone ringing."

"And how many people do you know named Duncan?" he asked.

"So do you think it's Bobby?"

"You're probably right. It being a wrong number. Sorry, I got over on you. Come here let me give you a hug."

"I think we can do better than a hug." I walked over and grabbed his arm and started towards the bedroom.

"Maybe later. I think I am going to keep walking. Keep spinning the ideas we talked about." He gave me a kiss and left for several hours. "You keep me inspired." Several times throughout the night, my arm swept across the empty space reserved for Duncan. It was about two in the morning when he slid into bed next to me, and I just pretended I was asleep.

The next morning, I left Duncan sleeping and a note saying I was having my morning tea and some scones at Peach's Cafe. I would be there for a bit and hoped he would join me before he went to class. I also reminded him we were having dinner with the professor and her husband tomorrow night and not to get too wrapped up in his writing.

At Peach's, I got my favorite spot in the back booth where the sun hit the windows and warmed up the spot by ten degrees. My head was in the newspaper when I spotted Duncan walk past. He ordered at the counter and was leaving without saying hi. Realizing he may not have spotted me in the back corner, I just jumped up, knocked the table, and spilled my tea. Half the cafe heard my commotion. Embarrassed and pant leg wet, I went to the front for some napkins and to reach Duncan before he was out the door. I tapped his shoulder, and he turned only for me to see it was not Duncan after all.

The similarity was in the eyes, but the square jaw and high forward made this guy look like a Hollywood A-list actor. I stepped back suddenly after realizing my mistake, but electricity shot through me. Maybe it was the similar features to Duncan, but something stirred inside me. Maybe because Duncan left me unsatisfied last night, but I wanted to jump this man right there.

Never had I had a wondering eye or stray thought while with Duncan or any previous boyfriend, but something cracked inside of me. I stood there like a pillar of salt from Sodom and Gomorrah. It was actually powdered sugar dusted all over me from when Ms. Clara had run into me with some pastries, but something had awakened inside of me.

The man's smile was gracious while the other customers, rightfully so, laughed. He handed me his napkin and retreated. Ms. Clara pulled me into the kitchen and handed me a rag, but that too was covered in powdered sugar so I retreated to the bathroom for a quick clean up under the electric hand dryer. While the powdered sugar floated all over the bathroom, my mind wandered back to the man.

Guilt washed over me, and I went to find Duncan. No cell phones in those days, so it was a guess if he was either writing in his campus dorm room, at class, or maybe at the university library. International students each had their own bedroom, shared bathroom, and small sitting area for four.

When we first got together as a couple, it was there in his room. We slept together fairly soon after meeting. I was hesitant to bring someone back to my place. I was proud of my home but also knew the dangers of living alone. But once a roommate of his recognized me as guest lecturer and had heard us having sex, I figured I was past the point in my life that confined me to sex on a dorm bed. We had known each other about a month. I finally thought it was safe to bring him to my place.

One of the flatmates was just leaving as I got there and let me into the suite. Three of the suite doors were shut including Duncan's. One student was at his desk with his head buried in a book. I knocked on Duncan's door but got no answer. I tried the door handle. The knob did not turn, but the door pushed back as it had not latched when Duncan closed the door when he'd left.

The room left me speechless. Papers were scattered everywhere. The bed was covered in books, notebooks, folders, including some of mine, loose paper, and dirty clothes. The closet nook was empty expect for a raincoat on the floor. The desk held more papers and an endless supply of open soda cans. The desk chair was just about the only thing not covered in a mess.

This was not the room of a sensitive yet methodical writer I knew. One critique I had given him was it had hit story points very well but some of his characters lacked depth, making them hard to connect with. There are rules to follow when doing creative writing, but his writing shouldn't reflect a checklist from a how-to-write-a-mystery pamphlet. I guessed he had finally let loose literally in his literature, and that is how he got the writing job.

I stepped out of his room so not to disturb anything and laughed at the idea of someone knowing if anything in the room "disturbed." The decision was made not to tell him about my visit.

Every writer has their own process. Who am I to pass judgment on others?

After my work at the high school and some good writing time in an empty classroom there, I decided to surprise Duncan with another of his favorite meals I cooked, a great American burger. Food in Europe is great, but food in Britain, at the time, was fair, and nothing beat a juicy burger cooked in your own backyard. I walked over to the grocery store to get all the fixings and ran into his professor.

Remember earlier when I said the professor talked about Duncan and I collaborating on stories? I had left my groceries, went for a long walk, and was running home when I gave you some background information. Well, here we are now, and I am running home getting blisters on my feet.

I am not a runner and was not dressed for a run, so I must have looked liked a maniac but didn't care. There was something about the two scenes that were playing over and over in my head. The chaotic scene of his room and my tidy office. Naturally, if you are looking for something you misplaced like a notebook or a folder, you would move things around. Not necessarily flip the room over, but things would get moved around unless you were looking for something and didn't want to be discovered.

The porch door practically flew off its hinges when I flung it open. The house door was locked. After Duncan moved in, he had insisted that door be locked. Why make it easy for a burglar? I laughed at the idea of crime in River Bend. The exception was sleeping alone at night as a female, I had always locked the door. I also understood the irony of sleeping on the porch. Sometimes, I can't make logic out of the things I say and do.

I scrambled for my key and finally dug it out. The climb to the office was slow. I hoped I was wrong and tried to run the different reasons with each step I took. To the left of the desk were four boxes of old writing material and research books. The collection of stories for the women's magazine were in the bottom box filed with my collection of short stories I'd pitched to my agent.

A friend had once suggested I get a metal filing cabinet instead of cardboard beer cases. I was insistent the metal cabinets were too mundane and boring looking for my office, and I liked the colorful boxes and they were the perfect size for my folders. And much cheaper, being free when purchasing a bottle of wine. I slid Miller Lite, Sam Adams, Miller High Life off of PBR. PBR was unusually light when I lifted it on my lap.

Before I flipped open the lid, I knew folders were missing papers. The professors words were echoing in my head, "collaborating." Or stealing? How similar were our stories or were they my stories?

How could he? I didn't have much proof, but let's not be dumb about it. I would give him the benefit of doubt, but high judgment was seething from me. Is this why he didn't want me reading his material lately? Most of these stories had yet to be published. I submit my material in full so I can move on to the next story. If "his" material were to be out there before my stuff, I could be ruined.

Was I jumping to conclusions? We all take inspiration from other's writing. I loved this man. We adored each other. I thought, *Let me talk to him before I make it more than what it is*.

Two hours later, I went to the high school book club I was an advisor for at the community library. So lost in my own thoughts, I approved the next book that would sure fire up some parents, but so be it. Let it be a lesson on free reading and learning.

I said earlier our only fight was when he had left for three days. What happened next wasn't so much a fight as an ending. He came to my house that evening. I couldn't then and realized I had never before called it our house; it was always my house. We shared our dreams and hopes but not my house. I was proud of what I had accomplished on my own.

Apparently, I had also shared my writing. At first, he denied it and tried to avoid the topic. I kept my voice even, never raising the volume. Anytime I wanted to scream, I squeezed a peanut in my hand. After twenty minutes, the floor of the kitchen looked like a dive bar at happy hour with free popcorn and nuts.

When I demanded he show me what he submitted to the publisher, he tried turning it into "our success" and how we could build a writing empire together and flood both the US and UK markets with our writing. I reminded him it was MY writing.

I asked why he did it. His writing was good enough to get him a full scholarship for a master's program in creative writing. The words "good enough" sliced through him. His body language shifted from rolled shoulders, puppy-eyed-groveling to black steel beady eyes.

"Good enough. That's right good enough, never will I be good, much less great. Hearing straight from the lady herself in her home in her town. I'm just her husband with no name for myself. Screw having a pen name when I never will have a name of own."

I crushed five peanuts I had balled in my fist. Anger had turned to fear. This man was speaking as if he were on a church pulpit spewing enteral damnation to those who don't believe his teachings. "You'll never be your brother, Duncan, nor do you need too. It is fine where you are. Don't need more."

He paced wildly around the room. I was not sure if he knew I was there. He was lost in his own head. He'd make his voice sound like what I thought might be his mother putting him down. He walked into the living room pulling things off the shelves. His skin was pasty white, and sweat beaded around his collar. A lamp was pushed over and cushions pulled from the couch.

I gasped in fear when he picked up a silver frame with our wedding photo in it. His head swiveled towards me. I couldn't recognize the man in front of me. I took a step back and knocked over a glass, and it shattered across the kitchen floor. The noise did not break his stride around the living room. While he paced around the room, I stepped out of his line of sight and eventually out the back door.

CHAPTER THIRTY-EIGHT

EG'S STORY - GETTING TO THE POINT OF IT ALL

I didn't even bother knocking on the door. My door may not have been locked, but at least it had a functioning lock. The professor's husband was In the recliner watching TV and gave me a nod before calling for the professor. She came from her sewing room, and with one look at me, she wrapped her arm around my shaking body, sat me down at the kitchen table, and started the teakettle.

"Do I need to call the police?" she asked, and her husband was suddenly beside her listening.

"No. Please, no. There is not much to tell the police."

"Are you hurt?" he asked.

"No!" I didn't want to be a victim. That is stupid I know. No one wants to be a victim. I didn't want any of this to be bigger than what it was. Let him burn out. It would be fine later. The man I loved would return. "I need just a moment to be here."

The professor led me to the couch, put a mug of tea in my hand, blanket on my lap, and a bowl of animal crackers next to me. They remained in the kitchen allowing me my space. Somehow, I managed to fall asleep and woke to the only light coming from the television. He was asleep in the recliner, and professor nowhere to be found.

The moonlight gave me a good look at the coyote crossing the street when I left their house around two a.m. I circled my house and peered in the living room window and saw Duncan on the floor curled up in a ball. I returned to my spot on the couch next door for several more hours.

I remained awake until around four, and when I woke at six thirty, the professor was in the kitchen, and her husband was nowhere to be found. My schedule was clear for that Saturday morning. I was handed a fresh mug of tea, and I could see from their kitchen window the lights were off in my house. The coffeepot was half-empty, which I took as a sign her husband was already at work.

"Thanks for the couch last night. I am going to miss you when you move out by the lake. To be honest, I won't miss that big ol' truck of yours that's older than me with an even older muffler. Maybe I will miss the truck. Hauling away all the yard debris is a breeze with a truck and having a husband who knows how to drive a manual. Any idea who the new buyers are? Would one happen to be a good

228

mechanic?" I asked. Now knowing the mechanic and dear friend moved in years later.

"A young couple. Don't think they will be here long. He is opening the new ARCON factory, and I can't see her adjusting to a town of this size. How about you? Still sticking around River Bend?"

"As of now, I can't imagine leaving. One day maybe, but not now," I answered.

"At least I see you're getting rid of that old propane tank for your heat. Don't know how those were ever allowed in a basement much less still operating these days. Excited about finally getting air-conditioning?"

"I am still budget-minded. Just new heating. Maybe in a year or two I will upgrade and get some air-conditioning," I said.

"Don't let them take you for too much money. You know my Pappy can remove the old tank. He might even want for it for scrap. Make it sort of a trade, labor for the metal," Professor said.

Good neighbors just helping neighbors, doing things without the exchange of cash, never being in debt to someone. Just doing the right thing to help the fellow man or in this case a neighbor.

Professor wasn't done speaking. "And—"

I raised my hand to stop her from asking what she didn't want to ask. "It was just an argument. I stepped away before it got too crazy," I lied.

She knew I lied. We let the lie sit there.

"Moving and early retirement for you. Big week," I said and got no reply.

Professor grabbed two cereal bowls, milk, and spoons and put them on the table. With her back to me, she pulled out three cereal boxes and said, "You know I was married before Pappy. All I am going to say is, you can't control who you love. That just happens inside you. What you can do is control what you do with that love."

That little nugget really smacked reality into my gut. Before I could respond, the front door flew open, and with a squeal of delight, we heard, "Pappy! Grandmama! Look what I made for you."

Professor got up to greet her granddaughter, and I slipped out the back door. Her phone rang, and I heard Professor Patty say, "Honey, give Grandmama a minute, I've been waiting on this call. EG, 7 p.m. dinner, but come over anytime before."

I stood briefly deciding if I wanted to go home. A walk was what I needed, but I felt like I was abandoning my home. Still, I needed to clear my head some more. The fall weather had hit hard, and there was talk of a rainstorm and severe weather hitting the area.

One quick walk to Peach's to get something warm. Professor had made me a tea drinker. She said all the coffee while writing will tear my insides apart. Green tea is so good for you, she would recite. Sometimes you do something just because you know the person will not let up so it is just best to go with what the hippie tells you to do.

It was a proud moment six months later when I got her to drink green tea with Jasmine. She pulled her long gray hair into floppy bun and just said, "Hmm, all these years of me adding fruit, oils, and other stuff, you find the perfect supplement in six months."

I was too timid at the time to ask her about "oils and other stuff." However, maybe the professor and the Grateful Dead had it right all along with living on reds and vitamin C because then at fifty-five she had the spirit and gusto of a twenty-five-year old. Right now, I felt like an exhausted fifty-five-year-old, thirty years my senior.

Without even thinking, I ordered hot chocolate before I realized I didn't have my wallet on me. Mrs. Clara hesitated for only three seconds before she hesitantly declared I was good for it, but she would expect the money tomorrow.

"Absolutely," I assured her.

Rapid-fire questions were zinging around my head. How much did Duncan plagiarize? Was it close to publication? What other lies are out there? Does plagiarism mean there is an evil core to the man? How am I going with live with someone who stole from me? It's worse than if he stole jewelry and pawned it. The words are mine. Things I have created from nothing. Without thought to me, he did the most selfish thing a spouse could do: he ignored me and what I was worth.

I was in the middle of the crosswalk when Professor's words liberated me. I may love the man, but what I do with that love is up to me. Me! Not my marriage license. Not his promises. Not his lies. ME, I get to decide.

I wish I'd had my troop, The EARLs, then. One year too soon before we met. A clean prospective would have made a world of a difference for everyone.

A car horn beep forced me out of the street and into a pros or cons list. What words did I need to hear him say? I immediately erased that thought. No words could undo what he had done. Then I thought, *Actions speak louder than words*. His previous actions had said a lot about the man. And his actions last night was as if he were a different man. If that happened once, what could stop it from it happening again?

I came home to a tidy, quiet house and a note with flowers that simply said, "Love you. Gone to write." The living room was cleaner than it had been twenty-four hours ago and everything in its place. Was everything ok? Had I overreacted at his outburst? Should anything excuse what he had done?

The upstairs room was usually my writing sanctuary, but I would go to the town's library to do my edits. Today, I was no mind frame for editing my current story, you need to be on point for that, and I was nowhere ready to eagle-eye my story. The weather was too crisp and misty for a walk, so I had no choice but head to the library. Saturdays mornings take on a whole new crowd. Kid story times were at different hours, and high school kids researching projects took up way too many tables. My head was chaos, and I didn't need that in my happy place.

Brian, the head librarian, saw me eyeing my favorite spot in the corner occupied by screaming kids. "Are you here to write or research?"

"Write and hide?" I don't know why I added the last part.

"Follow me."

He left the line at the desk and opened his office door. "It's not much and can be claustrophobic, but if you shut the door, you are in world by yourself."

"I appreciate this."

"The chair reaches around either side of the table," Brian said and left me just outside the room before he quickly returned to the library patrons.

Not sure what I expected the but word *office* was overrated; however, I found it was everything I needed. It held one table with a computer and three filing cabinets. The chair I can tell you had not been issued by the city. He must have brought it in himself. High-back, mahogany, old-school banker chair on wheels. It was currently facing a beige wall with a calendar and the library policy page pinned to a bulletin board. The two other beige walls soaked up the vibrant colors from the fourth wall. Floor-to-ceiling vintage album covers wallpapered the entire wall.

I dropped in the seat and lost myself in Led Zeppelin, Joe Cocker, Bellamy Brothers, and a kaleidoscope of others. Songs from each album I knew danced in my head with flashes from a high school dance and bonfires along the river, playing at my grandparents' house, bar time in college, and my first night I spent with Duncan in his on-campus room.

A tear fell from my eye, and I didn't know if it was sweet or sad. I had such great memories of songs I had not heard in years. They brought me so much joy.

Why do I have such mixed feelings about the man I love and married?

Should a simple sincere "I am sorry" cover stealing my work? How much did he take? Inspiration or copying? All that aside what about the man last night? He went from denial, defensive, turning my support for him into pity. The look in his eyes. The Duncan I knew disappeared.

Children shrieking down the hallway snapped me from my inner spiral. It was a crappy day outside, crappy mood inside me, which was a perfect formula for some good writing. I turned the chair to face a beige wall and wrote for hours.

Brian knocked on the door. "It seems this worked out for you. You missed the announcement that we are closing. Saturdays are a short day."

"Wow, it's one already? This place was a lifesaver. It may have salvaged my Saturday and freed up my Sunday with all the writing I just got done. I owe you one."

"Just keep the kids reading. Have you reconsidered doing any reading programs at the elementary or junior high school level?"

"You have got to let that idea go. My love is for writing, books, and talking about books. I am not a grade school teacher by any means. You saw the look of panic in my face when I realized it was toddler time."

"Keep an open mind," Brian asked.

"I will, if you will?" I said. "I got an old friend from camp coming to town next month. I was thinking of starting a book night at my house. I would love for you to join us. There will be a few others there from town. Her name, well, camp name is Trapper. We are reading that last one you suggested for me so I know you already read it so you have no reason not to come to dinner."

He rolled his eyes. "If you want me to keep an open mind, you will have to as well."

Strolling out of the library, I was going to keep an open mind about my husband. The sweet guy that runs to the store just before closing so I can have syrup with my pancakes in the morning. The guy climbed the roof to clean the gutters after four dates. The guy that totally lost it last night.

The afternoon storms were hitting on target. I would've known that if I had listened to the news anytime in the past two days.

"Let me guess, you walked here," Brian said. "C'mon, I will give you a ride, and you will have to explain why you picked that book to discuss. I got others I could recommend."

We ran to his car forty feet away, and my hair and feet were soaked. I had water running down my back, but my backpack with my writing was dry. We could hardly see ten yards in front of us. The windshield wipers were working so fast I thought they might fly off the car.

"You might as well do forty through the neighborhood. No one is crazy enough to be out in this weather," I said.

"Thank god you walk everywhere. This town is much safer for that if you think I can do forty in this rain. Hey, is that some guy running from your house. Duncan?"

"I can't tell if he came from my house or Professor's. Duncan doesn't have a jacket like that," I said.

"Where did he go?" Brian asked.

"No clue."

"Want me to come in with you? Check the house?"

"I know the weather is crap and the rainstorm is a perfect setting for a horror flick, but it's only one in the afternoon. We should be worried if the stranger wasn't running in this weather. Besides, its probably some fool trying to sell lawn treatments or the Lord."

"It's just weird either one of us doesn't recognize him."

"Recognize him? I barely saw the guy."

Brian backed into my driveway so the passenger door would be closer to the porch door. I couldn't help but think that man was the perfect match for Trapper. I ran to the porch and shook the rain from myself and unknowingly knocked off the note stuck in the door. It fell to the porch floor and under the sofa only to be found later, too late.

The house was quiet and empty. I had done some excellent writing this morning and knew I wouldn't get back in the groove, so I went to work

236

in the kitchen. A few times a year, I baked like I was a one-woman bake sale. I put the radio on and got to work. Scones, cookies, and banana bread.

Three hours later, Pappy knocked on the patio door and walked in. The knock was more of a courtesy as not to scare me. He only took one step in and said, "Professor sent me over to tell you come over anytime. This rain is not good for much besides eating and good company."

He was almost back on the patio before he shouted, "We will take a little of whatever you got baking."

CHAPTER THIRTY-NINE

EG's Story - Answers Are Coming Out.

Twenty minutes later, I pulled the last of the cookies out of the oven, changed my top for the third time that day, wrapped some baked goodies to take with me, and left a note for Duncan saying I went over early and join us when he got here.

I ran next door and let myself in without a second thought or one knock. Kicked off my rubber boots and hung the blanket I'd thrown over my head on a kitchen chair and plopped myself down in another.

"Still that bad out there, I see. Did you finally finish reading what I had set aside for you this morning?" Professor said and handed a glass of full of ice and brown liquor and patted my shoulder.

"You know I don't drink bourbon. Can I walk this in to Pappy?"

"Thought you might need it. Glad you came over. I'd sent him over to make sure we were good and hoped I didn't cross a line I shouldn't have." Professor saw the quizzical look on my face. "Didn't you read it? I could see you pounding away in the kitchen this afternoon. Just like your mama used to do when she was upset. Except she wouldn't bake, she would make stews, casseroles, and anything you could freeze."

That memory brought a smile to me. "After my dad bought that expensive fancy lawn mower when he retired and she thought their dream of moving to Florida was dead, I think she chopped for two days straight and cooked for another three. They have been down there three or four years now," I said.

"She cooked so much she could have opened a food pantry that week. I probably still have thing of beef stew in that freezer downstairs. I'll bring it over when we move in a week." We both laughed knowing it might be true.

"I was only baking to warm up the house. Get the dampness out. What did you drop off? I didn't see anything."

"Just a note saying I got something for you and to come get it. I just assumed you came and got it. Left it right here on the kitchen counter. A manila envelope with your name on it," Professor said.

"Never saw it? Is it dirt on the people buying this house? Are they wanted for murder in three states?" I laughed, but the professor didn't.

The rain was pelting the windows matching my heart beat. She couldn't be confirming what I feared. I took a long pull of the bourbon and let it burn on the way down.

"I had my suspicions last semester that something wasn't right, and from our conversation in the grocery store, I don't think you knew either. Thinking that maybe you've been helping or coaching him. Maybe I'm fine accepting some of his work, but it was too much. Been waiting to say something until I knew for sure."

"It goes back that far? Last semester." I was barely speaking above a whisper. "Not just for this inquiry for a real paying job?"

Professor had both her hands around her mug of tea. She stood up and poured herself a bourbon straight. "It's worse than that."

"How could that be?" Not sure if I said that out loud. Plagiarism is just not cheating. It's stealing someone's thoughts, ideas, soul-produced creations. Copying an answer on a multiple-choice test is cheating on your score; it is not stealing from someone. Plagiarism is robbing them of their creativity.

"I don't think, well, I know it's just not your work," Professor said.

There was nothing to say so I just let her continue. "His writing has been erratic lately. I'm not just talking about the usual student who get gets positive feedback on two writing assignments and decides they're the next Salinger or Vonnegut and goes off on some esoteric journey and thinks the next Pulitzer is theirs for the taking. Some of his writing is brilliant but not consistent. This is a competitive master's program to get into. I told him he should reflect on his writing that got him into the program. Stick to what you know, build off that, and you don't have to recreate the wheel.

"I think from the look on your face he never talked to you about this. When I mentioned for him to reflect on his past work, it was like he transferred into another person. I pulled his writing submissions so I could see what the selection committee liked about his work. He was a late add to the program. International students tend to be because it's a slow process and all the extra legal paperwork. All the writing submissions were hand written. Next fall, everything will be on the word processors. I am explaining these details so you understand I am not guessing at what I am saying.

"His submission work is completely done in a different hand. The handwriting is different from his work once he started here. He entered the college with someone else's work. It just didn't start with your work."

"She is absolutely right," Duncan said.

I jumped in my seat. We hadn't heard him come in the back door. Patty did not move. Her hands fixed around her mug, and her eyes met Duncan's and then mine. He was holding flowers. "These are for you, Professor."

Patty didn't move."You can put them by the sink."

He shook off his coat and shoes, gave me a peck on the cheek as he walked over to the sink. I didn't move. He took the kitchen chair between us at the table. "My writing career is not what I hoped it would be. Need to move on. There is no point in doing what I can't. Professor, I can't thank you enough for making me refocus.

"I owe my lovey wifey a most sincere apology. Never meant for you to think I would take what is yours. Tried using your writing as inspiration for my own, but I guess I took a little too much." He stood up. "Pappy, my mate, get in here."

We waited for Pappy to pull himself from the recliner. "Make sure you grab your pint, mate."

Pappy walked in with his can of Miller, and Duncan got himself a glass with a heavy pour of bourbon. "Today has been liberating. Professor, I am sure you have seen many a grad student flounder. I did it with the best of them. I am thankful for you taking me out of my hole and showing me I can't go on like that. I would like to thank my wifey for choosing me. We built something wonderful together, and we are going to see the world together as we planned. You can continue to write, and I will be there for you and carve my out my new path. I know one might not be happy when leaving a fine master's program like this, but I see it as relief. We have room for only one writer in our family. Let's toast to new beginnings and surprises."

"More surprises?" I hadn't lifted up my glass yet to meet Duncan's outstretched arms.

"We are going away for a few days. Hide away from this rain. Go like we talked about. It's not far but that little inn over in Woodward. Sleep in, indulge in the weekend brunch, and take whatever class they're offering tomorrow, candle making or maybe to learn to knit. Who knows, maybe I will find inspiration for my next path. Maybe get a job working at inns across the country. You write and I do the work. To new beginnings."

He clinked his glass to mine and came in for another kiss. He turned to Professor, and she tilted her mug as a salute to him but never clinked his glass.

Pappy matched his beer to Duncan's glass. "My, oh my, I never met a fellow so eager to start new." Pappy roared with laughter. "Good for you. Hope you're not running off before you have some of Professor's seven-hour oven pot roast."

Pappy slapped Duncan on the back and bourbon spit out of him. There was nothing to do but laugh.

"What do you say, can your new life start in an hour or so?" Pappy asked again.

Duncan hesitated only a second before agreeing. "Right on. Of course we were invited for dinner tonight."

"Good, good, good. Maybe while we eat I can persuade you to help out for a few days at the store and with our move for bit unless you find your path in the next forty-eight hours there. I need someone that can drive my manual truck. Kids here these days never learn that skill. Few a trips day, picking up some inventory for the store."

"Sure, I can drive that truck for you. It's just a matter if I can remember the proper side of the road." The men laughed together.

Professor got up and opened up the oven, and a heavenly scent of roast beef and potatoes blanketed the room. My shoulders dropped, and my back slouched when I watched Professor pull plates from the cabinet. If she thought it was fine to go on with dinner, I should be fine.

"The dinner does smell wonderful. Let me help set the table, Professor. Well, I guess from now on, it's just neighbor, Patty and still Pappy Phil."

I watched Duncan retrieve the items following Professor's instructions. He dropped two knives barely missing his little toe. "You see a ghost outside that window? What's got you so clumsy?" Pappy asked twice before Duncan answered.

"Just surprised to see someone out in rain. Thought someone was pulling into our driveway, but they just turned around."

Dinner was a blur for me. Professor's words earlier were muffled by Pappy and Duncan talking American football. Phil having to explain some of the rules multiple times for Duncan to get smidge of understanding of the game. Duncan tried interjecting soccer and rugby into the equation and Pappy would have to repeat everything again. After a second helping of pot roast for everyone, Duncan managed to get a large laugh from Professor and me when he simply asked, "So the high scores wins."

Pappy laughed. "I guess that is all you need to know."

"This was amazing dinner, Prof, I mean Neighbor. That is very American, *Neighbor*. I like it. I hope EG is ok if we skip out of dessert. Anxious to get to the inn," Duncan said.

"That new path is waiting for you," Pappy encouraged.

Professor was quiet during dinner, and I didn't get my usual hug when leaving one of her Saturday-night meals. Their house phone ringing prompted the quick exit in the rain. We ran into the house, and I nearly tripped over a For Sale sign.

"What is that doing in our yard?" I screamed in the howling rain when I ran into the porch.

Duncan answered, "The wind must have knocked it down, and when I came over, I put it up but didn't realize where I was when I jammed in back in the ground."

"Should we move it back?" Just then lightning struck, and both of us burst into laughter. "I guess neither one of us needs to pick up a metal frame in the dark and move it twenty feet right now."

"Besides, it says 'Sold' so no one needs to inquire about the house or whose in it?" Duncan said.

"Whose in it? You mean like who is selling the house?" I asked.

"That or who is lingering around. Would you buy a house if the sellers said they believed it was haunted or that granny croaked in the kitchen?" Duncan asked.

"Interesting question. Know it shouldn't matter but probably not. You are a creative mind. Don't give up on writing."

He dropped his eyes and didn't respond.

I grabbed a duffel bag and threw some clothes in it. You already packed?"

He nodded towards his suitcase.

"You're bringing a whole suitcase for the night? Wanna toss some things in here? Make it light." I realized then he only had a suitcase worth of clothes.

"Maybe we make it two nights, a week, or two weeks," Duncan boasted.

"So excited for your new adventure, but I have deadlines and work on Monday."

"Start packing. You can write anywhere. Take Monday off and start my new adventure with me. We can't be living off of just your income, or are you trying to keep me a kept man?"

"Speaking of income, the idea of a getaway is interesting, and a place with a fireplace and good room service sounds inviting, but how are we paying for this? I ordered the new heating system for the house."

Duncan stopped moving around like a toddler. "Since Professor made sure I am not a student anymore, I will use the last of my stipend for the room."

"You paid for it already?" I asked.

"Well, I used the credit card to secure the room and said we would pay cash upon departure."

He meant my credit card. His behavior was confusing. How could someone be in such a good mood while losing what he said was his passion? His writing was what I had first found remarkable about him. The characters and worlds he built inside his stories made him seem like a creative, inventive, and worldly thinker. Getting to know the man that created something out of nothing was a real turn-on for me. If he could just get that back.

I turned on the living room and porch light. Duncan said I should leave them off. "I don't subscribe to the theory to leave lights on while you are gone. A burglar just has to drive through a neighborhood during the day and whatever porch light is still on at noon tells you the people are gone for a long period of time. A dark house at night just means you are out for the night and could return anytime."

We heard a knock on the porch door, and Pappy entered without waiting for an ok from me. "I think you should take the truck if you are still set on heading to Woodward tonight. EG, you got to get a new car or least new tires before the snow hits this season. This rainstorm is predicted to turn into an ice storm. Those country roads could be a mess the next few days. We're both home tomorrow so we won't miss it."

"That generous of you," I said.

"Well, my honey said it, we don't need your mother coming after us if something were to happen to you. Duncan, look forward to working with you if you want it."

Pappy was gone before we could argue the moot point. There was a reason my mother had spread her food around. It was a prepayment of sorts for watching out for my sister and me after they'd left for Florida and for heaven a few years later.

Duncan grabbed my car keys and moved my car into the garage before he rushed me next door to Pappy's truck. The engine roared to life like the thunder outside. My husband, who I felt love, anger, and pity for backed out of their driveway. I turned away from him to sort out my feelings. I looked at my house pitch-black with the curtain drawn and sold sign in the front yard, and it left me feeling vacant.

CHAPTER FORTY

EG's Story - Winding Down or Building Up.

I woke up to the sound of someone pounding on the door and failed to realized where I was for a moment. My arm slid across the flannel sheets to an empty right side of the bed.

"Ms. Graham, this is . . ."

I missed the name of person at the door when I stubbed my toe on the base of the three-foot-tall brass owl statue and shouted something vulgar enough the person at the door should have retreated. The wool throw blanket acted as a robe as I opened the door to a hotel employee and a police officer in uniform with water and mud seeping from his shoes.

"What is going on?"

"Ms. Graham."

"Please call me EG."

"Yes, of course. May we come in?" the officer said.

The room at the inn had a sitting area with a love seat in front of a gas fireplace and a recliner. Hours earlier, Duncan and I had fallen asleep on the sofa. The conversation on our forty-minute ride to the inn was mostly about the conditions and possible theme of our room. I kept the conversation light. Not sure about my feelings for my husband and didn't want to get into it while we were on the road.

Kitschy inns in the country could always be counted on for a theme. Maybe on general theme of the whole place or each of the forty rooms have their own. I went with birds and presidents. Duncan laughed. "You Americans sure had a thing for the early presidents. The old white guys we dismissed, you all put them on pedestals. My vote is deer, deer, and more deer." It was such a sweet laugh to listen to while I sorted out my feelings.

The officer dismissed the hotel employee with a simple head nod, and a female officer followed him. I hobbled towards the recliner.

"Before we speak to you, ma'am, can we see some identification?" Officer One said.

"Ah, sure. What's going on?" I went to the nightstand for my purse, and it was then I realized

Duncan was not in the room. I had known he wasn't there before I opened the door, but I felt his absence now. My hand was shaking when I handed the officer my license.

"You ok ma'am?" Officer One said.

"Not really. It's six in the morning. I stubbed, possibly broke my toe. My husband is not here, and I have two officers talking to me while I am in my pajamas. None of this could be good, so can you get right to it."

The female officer stepped forward and held out her arm towards the chair. I followed her lead and sat down.

"I am Officer Kat Connelly."

"Better tell me what room! Otherwise, I'm knocking on every door. I am the one that sent the officers here." We heard Professor making a fuss down the hallway. She stopped at the open door, and I told the officer to let her in. He dismissed the hotel employee for the second time, closing the door this time.

Professor sat on the arm of the chair I was in and held my hands.

"There is no good way to say this, but we believe your husband, Duncan, was in a auto accident and . . ."

CHAPTER FORTY-ONE

EG's New Reality.

The officers told me a truck skidded off the road and plunged into a ditch and ended up in a fireball. It is now to believed the man driving was Duncan. The fire was so intense they are only assuming at this point. She went on to explain they had gone to Professor's house thinking Pappy was driving. A farmer, an acquaintance of theirs, was up at that hour because one of his cattle was birthing, and he heard that muffler drive past. A few minutes later, he saw the fire and called 9-1-1.

The cab on the bed of truck came off while rolling down the hill, and with that, items tossed across the hill helped identify the owner of the truck.

Professor sat there hugging me and saying she was so grateful I was ok. "I knew in my bones you were still here. Told them we insisted you take the truck on account of the road conditions. I had to see it for myself. Couldn't be two of you in that truck, just couldn't be. Had to come see myself. Oh Lord, what would I tell your sister. This town would be devastated by it. Let me guess, you got into a fight, and he stormed off. Bless your heart, honey. Why did he have to go out in that storm? Just lucky you didn't go chasing him."

I sat there stunned. Professor sitting so close was making me claustrophobic. "Are you sure?"

The officer waited several beats before she continued, "The coroner will make the final decision. This is not going to be easy to hear. We are still at the scene, and I can only tell you what we know so far. The fire was intense. More than most car fires, due to the fact of some of the stuff that was in the bed of that truck. Again, this very early into the investigation." From her pocket, she pulled out a plastic bag with a red seal on it. "Can you identify this?"

I shook my head. "That is Duncan's watch."

Patty got up to retrieve the box of tissues. Tears were streaking down my face.

Last night, the conversation had been intentionally light. It was sweet when he saw the tea in the room was not my favorite and went to exchange it for me. We laughed when I turned on the television to some arena football game on, and we realized there was more football to learn. I was still upset with him, but the love was still there.

We had fallen asleep on couch and woke up to the hotel phone ringing. Duncan picked it up and said someone dialed the wrong room number. I remember crawling into bed, and the next thing I knew, someone was pounding on the door, and now I was looking at his watch.

My mind went to logic when staring at the plastic bag the officer held up. "You were able to retrieve this from the fire? If you got this, then you must be able to see him. You know for sure?" My eyes floated between the two officers. The lady officer had been doing all the speaking. She waited a beat before saying, "This might be too much for you."

"Tell me. NOW!"

"This one can handle it," Professor said.

"Again, this is only the preliminary findings, but we think that when the truck rolled over part of his arm was severed through an open window or possibly from the car door if he was trying to jump from the vehicle."

I'm not sure about much after that. Professor talked to the officers more than me. She packed my things and led me to her car. The ride home was long and quiet. Thinking back now, she must have gone the long way to avoid the crash scene.

We pulled into their driveway that separated our two houses.

"Come on in, dear," Professor said.

"I think I just want to be alone."

"Hon, you need to come in." I could see her touching my arm but couldn't feel anything. She looked me in the eye. "There is more. A lot more. You need to hear this now before you answer any more questions."

We walked in the kitchen, and I sat down at the same spot I was just at fourteen hours prior. Professor turned on the teakettle and pulled out some fresh mugs and put them on the table along with a tray of cookies, scones, and banana bread I had brought over just the previous night. We didn't speak while we waited for the water to boil. She grabbed a wool blanket from the living room and wrapped it around my shoulders, and she finally spoke after our tea bags were steeping.

"Hon, I don't know how to tell you all this so I am just gonna get it all out there. I started to tell you some of this before, but well . . . oh hell, I just, well, oh. So much for me being a English professor when I can't even start. What do I tell the kids . . . just out with it.

"So, Duncan's class writing was different than his submission essays. I compared the writing, and not only was the tone and style different, it was different handwriting. He was either stealing work now or cheated his way into the program.

"I made some calls to two of his undergraduate teachers that wrote letters of recommendation. One teacher said she never wrote such a letter, and the other one was confused as she thought Duncan didn't accept the program in the States. She had just run into him last month, and he mentioned his work with Britain's military. Either the Royal Navy or Air Force,

258

she couldn't remember because she was surprised with someone being as talented as he was the military was not a logical step for the man.

"This wasn't making any sense so I dug a little deeper, and after a lot of inquiries, I spoke to his brother. It's best you hear it from him."

She stood up, walked into the living room, and left me processing what she'd said. It was as if I was listening to a delayed report. Although she left the room ten seconds prior, I was just hearing the words now and watched Pappy shuffle in. He couldn't or wouldn't meet my eye.

Following behind him was the man from Peach's yesterday. The man that had caught my attention and stopped me in my tracks. If I was breathing before, I definitely wasn't now.

CHAPTER FORTY-TWO

The man sat down across from me and introduced himself. "I am your husband's brother, half brother to be precise. The man you know as your husband is actually Robert Morgan. I am Duncan Morgan. Robert has used my name, likeness, and work history to come to the States.

"From the look on your face and everything Mrs. Cordon has told me, I understand this is all new to you. Not only did you lose your husband last night, you also lost the person. I don't know what stories and lies Bobby has told you, and it doesn't matter. All I can do is tell you the truth now.

"I am three years older than Bobby. My father left my mother and me when I was two. I have not seen him since. Bobby's father died when he was three and I was six. Our mother has addiction and mental health issues. Our childhood was anything but pleasant, and Bobby struggled to fit in anywhere. Our mother pitted us against each other to make us like her more. Bobby had multiple issues from not attending school for weeks on end, stealing things, and blaming others for his misfortune. His level of intelligence is high, but he cannot cope with stress or everyday problems very well.

"I was the one to apply for the master's program here. My time in the Royal Air Force was coming to an end, and I was considering all my options. One possible direction was furthering my education. At the last minute, I decided to continue my military career. All my correspondence was sent to our mother's flat. When he wasn't bunking on friends' couches, Bobby was living there while attempting to make a go of it at the university. Some of this is just conjuncture, but I think he decided to start over as me. Or least take the scholarship. Mrs. Cordon may have more insight on what happened at the college."

I didn't even realize they were still in the kitchen with us. Professor put fresh hot water in my teacup, which I hadn't touched, and laid a hand on the man's shoulder. "Finish your story, and I can fill in later although there is not much to add after you."

"I was alerted that something was up when my routine background check was flagged. Details are not important, but the most telling sign was my missing passport, and through a connection with the Ministry of Defense, I learned it was matched for a US-bound flight.

"A few months ago, I had mum moved into a care home. I believe here you call it a nursing home. I'd been paying her previous caregiver, Lilith, to clean out the flat. Just know, I trust Lilith and have no reason to doubt what she has found and not found in the house. I kept very little at the house. Partly having to do with having very limited emotional attachment to anything from childhood and having very little. I had left behind several boxes of stuff from my university days before I joined the Royal Air Force. Part of my mother's mental illness is her distrust of government, but with that, she kept a secure box with any government, church, and school communication. She even has a diary of date and time items were delivered to the home and who the mail carrier was that day.

"As I said, I trust Mrs. Lilith. All the correspondence with Jameson College and two other colleges in Connecticut are gone with some other material. Between the alert on my background check, speaking with Mrs. Lilith, and Bobby not being seen in the neighborhood for a long period of time, I went to the house to look for some answers. I happened to be there when Mrs. Cordon tried ring my mum. We got to talking, and we started putting things together.

"I'm sorry to tell you all this, but I believe a person has a right to know the good and bad," Duncan finished.

All eyes were on me.

"Oh," I said. That was not the most profound or insightful thing to say, but really what should be said after all that? I said. "This is a lot to follow in a short amount of time. I feel like I'm reading and making a recipe one step at a time not knowing what I'm making or when it's done. I gathered the ingredients, mixed up a lot of shit, and don't like what's coming out of the oven."

No one moved in the kitchen.

I spoke again, "Sorry, that was a weird analogy."

"I think that makes perfect sense," Professor said.

"It works for me," said the man across from me. "Please ask me any questions."

Professor tapped Pappy on the arm and started towards the living room.

"Please stay, if you like. I don't want to burden you more, but I may need someone to repeat this all to me later."

"Of course, darling," she said and they sat down.

The man said, "I can't apologize for someone's else behavior and trickery, but I am sorry for what he put you through."

"I appreciate that. My mind is swirling, and the only thing I can think to ask is about the writing. I read some of the early work your brother had written but now I wonder if that was your work."

"It might have been. I know the two careers of writing and combat training do not always go hand in hand, but those have been my two passions. I am an avid reader mostly of historical

264

nonfiction and, of all things, comics. A psychologist would probably have a field day with that, and throw in my childhood, that could get me my own page in a some medical magazine.

"My first degree, or what you call undergraduate degree, was history with a minor in creative writing."

"You can stop explaining British terms, we get it."

"It's part of the training to make sure everything is understood. Sometimes, it is hard to step out of it," the man across the table said.

"The stories about a teenager going back in history to create chaos you wrote?"

"Yes, ma'am."

"First off, your writing is incredible and inspiring. If your military skills match your writing skills, then Britain will be well served by you. Second, let's get one thing straight, you better not call me ma'am again. It's EG."

"Understood," he said.

"Were you at my house earlier? During the storm?"

"I was looking for my brother. I left a note."

"I do have another question that I never would have thought I would need to ask anyone." I could feel three sets of eyes on me, and I held the stares from the three of them in the room and finally asked, "So, Duncan Morgan, does this mean you and I are married?"

CHAPTER FORTY-THREE

BACK TO CLAUDIA'S STORY. IN A HOSPITAL.

Instructions were thrown out at random times. Jokes were made. Promises were expected to be followed through or otherwise some serious haunting would occur. Why did Sherrie think she would get so much say in the funeral?

Minimal church service, only if the parents insist.

Celebration of life should have a spiritual quality to it.

After party at the house for those that matter the most.

Location near the river and trail.

Not all the ashes should be spread in one spot.

No long speeches, it should not turn into a roast unless it's later in the night back at the house.

No memorial run-a-thon, bike-a-thon, fish-a-thon.

The conversation about names was fairly easy.

CHAPTER FORTY-FOUR

Tears were trickling down my face when Pete's parents walked in the room. Peggy stopped short, and Don ran into her. She only moved when Pete turned his head, and she saw his eyes open.

Don spoke first, "Claudia, the tears frightened us."

"Just tears of joy. He's been awake about twenty minutes. His doctor left and said all good but is still monitoring his heart and temperature. Watching for infection still. I knew you were on your way, otherwise I would've called."

Peggy went to Pete's left side and kissed his forehead while her kitting needles poked his chest.

She pulled out a tissue from somewhere and wiped tears away from her eyes.

"Good news, this one is going to marry me," Pete said.

Don looked at me, and I understood his concern. "Memory is fine for the most part. Right before the accident is fuzzy. He wants a hospital room wedding."

"Oh," Peggy and Don said in unison.

Later, I learned Peggy's short reply was due to lack of a church ceremony, and Don needed a moment to absorb that fact of what that really meant.

"Don't you want to see Claudia walk down the aisle at St. Marks?" Peggy asked Pete. "Well, we can have Father William come here if that is necessary."

"We can do that later," Pete said.

"Do you want to wait until you get released and have it in the backyard where your father planted the trees when you were born?"

"It's also where Doodles is buried so no," Pete said. "Why wait? It's not about the production and hoopla."

Don, ever so pragmatic, said, "Claudia, are you ok with all this, or are you letting my son bully you? Can't image you dreamed of this for your wedding setting. Let's file the paperwork and see how fast this can actually happen. You might be out by the time you can figure out how to do a marriage license."

"Thank you for looking out for me, Don. I can walk down any aisle at anytime. Right now, I just want him to smile and have some joy, and if that involves marrying him, I'll make the sacrifice." I laughed and squeezed Pete's hand. I hadn't realized how hot he was. *His temperature must be up again.* I tried to leave to call the nurse back in, but he wouldn't let go.

"Where is my phone?" Pete said.

"We don't know. We assumed it dropped in the fire. Who are you calling?" I asked.

"Your parents. Let's get on with this wedding. When can Katie Lyn and Matthew Middleton get here to marry off their daughter?"

"I am all for this wedding, but can we get through one day of you being awake? I will have Jenna find out what we need and if we can get Judge Lobel to perform the ceremony."

"Let my dad take care of the paperwork. We will probably have to dig up my birth certificate and whatever."

"Fine, but he's not picking my dress."

That got a chuckle out of Don and Pete. Peggy was too stunned to react.

"I'm gonna get Cheryl back in here and check your temperature," I said.

Cheryl was gone, and I spoke to a different nurse about having someone look at Pete again. I walked towards the lounge, and I saw the door to the stairwell and slipped inside.

The heavy door clinked shut, and I sat on the step and cried. Put my head into my hands, and my body shook. Somebody walked past, and I didn't care.

Someone else or the same person came back and sat next to me. I continued to look down but could see he was wearing scrubs and holding a tissue box. "Solitude or need to talk?"

"He doesn't think he is going to make it," I said.

"What do you think?" the man asked.

"It doesn't matter what I think. I just don't want him to be right this time."

"Wish I had some words of wisdom for you. Here keep the box." He was gone before I could say thank you. I called my mom and told her about Pete waking up and the new plans for the wedding.

"Darling, that's wonderful. Tell us what you need for the wedding, we are on it. I want in on this, please don't let Sherrie do it all." She laughed. "I get off early, and we can dress shop tonight. I will see what I can find on my lunch break."

Her enthusiasm was overwhelming and grounded me to the joy of a wedding regardless of why the date was so rushed. I was due to work that

272

evening and was fine going to the hotel. It was a piece of normal. For more normalcy, I called Sherrie and explained everything. Before I finished the last sentence, she interrupted to tell me she had to go so she could talk to my mom and coordinate things. I wondered if I would get to have any say in my wedding.

The rest of the morning, the hospital staff battled his temperature. Then things turned concerning with Detective Angie Decorah came in with questions. She wanted to question Pete alone. Don, Peggy, and I were not happy that she was ready to drill Pete.

"I am just gathering the facts."

"My son is a hero. He ran back into the store to pull people out. How can anyone say anything else?" Peggy said.

Even in his semi-sleepy state, Pete rolled his eyes. "Ma, it's fine. I get it. I don't have much to tell you that I can remember." Pete lifted his right hand, which held the nurse call button. He may have thought that was the pain medicine button. "Best I can say is I was at the house."

"Which house?" asked the detective.

"Claudia's."

"Is this the house from the previous incidents?"

"Yes, ma'am."

"Go on."

"I remember talking to Phil in his store. And heat. I remember heat and the noise."

A nurse came and said there were too many people in the room. Don and Peggy reluctantly left.

"So you talked to Phil."

Pete nodded yes.

"Anyone else?"

"I don't know. Just the yelling," Pete said.

"What were you talking about?"

"I don't know." Again Pete raised the nurse call button remote but did not press any buttons.

"Why do you think you would go see Phil at that hour during the day?"

"I don't know."

"Possibly to talk to him or Patty about Claudia's accident?"

"Could be an option or I wanted paint swatches," Pete said, and no one laughed.

"Phone records show your last incoming call was from EG Graham. Could that be the reason for the visit?"

Pete didn't lift up his arm when he answered this time. "Don't remember. Ask her."

"I am asking you."

"How long did we talk?" Pete asked.

"Your phone should tell you that. Where is your phone?"

"We think he dropped it in the store. The last pinged location was the store, but I am sure you know that," I said.

Agent Decorah asked, "Anything you want to add?"

"I really don't have much to tell you. If something comes to mind I will . . . I will tell you." His words were heavy. He tried wiping the sweat off his forehead, but the hospital ID bracelet caught a small burn mark on his forehead. He winced in pain and waved away any assistance. "Can, can you tell me what happened?"

"Still trying to piece it together, sir."

"What did the fire report say?" I asked.

"I don't have the final report," Agent Decorah said.

"But you do know some . . . something." Pete's breathing was labored.

"There is stuff you're not telling us?" I said.

"I know a lot of things, but nothing is concrete at this point. Just gathering information."

"Is Pete being accused of something?" I asked.

"There was an explosion and fire. Everything is being looked at. When more memory comes back, be sure to give me a call. I'll be back." She dropped her card on the bedside table and left.

Pete was tired but awake.

"Before your parents come back in, tell me what you didn't say to the detective," I said.

"I really don't remember much more than that. Did you talk to EG? I guess I did," Pete said.

"Sort of. She had an incident too. Not as bad as you."

Pete's heart monitor was beeping more.

"Take it easy. She is fine, but she fainted and hit her head."

"She is on her way back here. My mom talked to the husband of one of the hikers. I may have fainted, I don't know if it was exhaustion or something else. I think she gets in tomorrow, later tonight. The days have been a blur. She tried calling me but I missed it cause I was at work, so I guess she called you." I bent down and whispered, "You don't remember if you talked about what we found?"

"Found?"

I just nodded and waited for Pete to remember the basement. I know the room was not bugged by the detective nor did I think she was outside the room trying to eavesdrop, but I was still spooked by the bones. "In the basement, found."

Pete closed his eyes, drew a short breath and slowly spoke, "I explained the situation as delicately as I could. I heard her say, 'Patty.' It was definitely 'Patty' and then some noise like she dropped her phone. That's it or that's all I remember."

I feared his parents would come in any second. "There was some kid asking for money at the house."

"What do you mean?"

"Sherrie was home. The kid kinda cleaned up the yard and said he wants his money."

"Jordon? High school kid?"

"Didn't get a name, but high school age maybe sounds right from Sherrie's description."

"Give him the cash."

"Sherrie gave him some but didn't know how much or if the story was legit."

"You and the kid . . . ?"

The nurse and Peggy walked in, ending our conversation.

"Talking kids, first marriage and now kids. Busy morning, you two."

"Just asking if he was kidding about a hospital wedding."

"All right, now I need to change some of the bandages around the burn. This will not be pretty. You might want to leave or look away."

"Staying put." I'd hope Peggy would leave, but she just sat down and began knitting.

"We want to get you to get up and moving but not before some of the skin heals. Rest up and let's wait for what the doctors says." She was quick and tender yet she couldn't do anything about the smell. I didn't realize what was trapped below the bandages.

"Did Don go get something to eat?" I asked Peggy.

"I hope not," answered the nurse. "There is a food delivery address to the family and nurses on Pete's floor. This also came with a schedule for the next three days. Come here and pull the card from my pocket.

I walked over and pulled the index card from her pocket while she worked on Pete. "I guess when the person delivering the food went to pick it up, someone asked where the party was. The driver said hospital for the Morris family and staff. That customer said the guys at the plant will take care of tomorrow's lunch and several others piped in."

Today's lunch was from Jim and the guys from Draw bar; tomorrow was Don's old company; the day after was from the Jones family, and money-hungry Jacob said the guys from Pete's softball team would take the next day if he was still in the hospital. Katie, the morning server, took control and set up a calendar and collected money.

"I think I finally have an appetite, but Peggy help yourself first. I want to learn how to change the bandages."

"Nearly done here. Maybe next time," The nurse said.

I was trying to get more time with Pete alone to finish our conversation about the kid, weed, and switchblade. Just a typical conversation with my fiancé.

Peggy never left the room. My spirits were high, but my concern was skyrocketing along with his high temperature.

Work that evening felt normal, and I was wickedly efficient. Nervous energy had me deep cleaning the back office, and I gave everyone working something new to do. I suddenly had a motto that evening: keep moving or I will move you out of a job. Some found this fun, and a only a few were put off by my "life is too short so make of the most of it" attitude. Either you are with me or against your job. Maddie had to tell me to transfer my nerves into something better before I offended the wrong person. I had to explain if I sat down for one minute I would either fall asleep or start crying.

My mother came through at the right time. I channeled my nerves into excitement as I flipped through the photos she texted. She found three old classic wedding dresses in my size at our favorite vintage shop in St. Paul.

Maddie pushed me out the door at eight p.m. after I told a guest who was not happy with the view that the other option is the hotel across the street. I'd tried telling Maddie I was the manager and she was the employee, but she defended her

stance and said if I didn't leave, she would get
Sherrie in here to drag me out and that would be a
bigger scene but I would still have my job.

CHAPTER FORTY-FIVE

AFTER A FUNERAL, SHORTLY AFTER I FINALLY GOT OFF THE COUCH ON THE PATIO.

Between a florist shop and bike shop was a glass door with three company names scrolled across in gold script. I walked past the door twice each time getting a glimpse of the carpeted stairwell. Situated between the state capital and Camp Randall Stadium is this non-memorable door and about seven coffee shops, some with better bathrooms than others.

Drinking coffee, peeing, and walking were my stall tactics. I managed to pee or drink in all seven coffee shops before I finally had the courage to pull open the glass door. Suite B would lead me to either a title company, CPA's office, or tailor.

Suite B was to the right of the center stairwell, and at the end of the hall was a wood door with a small metal placard telling me I had arrived at Suite B. A six-inch window ran along the side of the door looking into a small reception desk.

The sign behind the women sitting at the desk read "Smith & Madison Title Company." I pushed open the door and surveyed the area before taking another step. The small conference room to the right was empty as were the six chairs in the waiting area. The room was clear of any dust and clutter as it made room for burgundy carpet that along with the artwork was straight from the '90s.

"Miss Middleton, welcome. I need you to read and sign this form."

I hadn't introduced myself nor her to me. I took longer than needed to sign the form. I needed another minute and maybe another coffee but settled for reading the form. I decided to just get on with whatever was waiting for me. I followed her down the hall to what could be described as a janitor closet. There was a brown door with scuff marks at the bottom, and at the three-foot level a large garbage can pressed into to open the door.

The lady held up her watch to the ordinary looking doorknob, and I heard a click. She stepped forward and held the door for me. There was a man in a suit standing at a reception area, but unlike the previous room, this reception was straight from

Architecture Digest. High-polish wood floors, leather Chesterfield sofas, several large televisions showing what the markets were doing in New York, London, Tokyo, and Hong Kong.

I would like to tell you what I felt, but I am not sure I was feeling anything at that point. My mind remembers the scent of a pleasant blend of rose and mint.

"Thank you, Ms. Jones. Claudia, come into my office, and all your questions will be answered. Let me first hand you this card so we can get started. Would you like any coffee, tea, or a cocktail perhaps?"

CHAPTER FORTY-SIX

PETE'S LAST FEW DAYS IN THE HOSPITAL.

Two days after my second proposal and two days before my wedding, I woke in the hospital room sometime after six a.m. I had gotten pretty good at sleeping through the routine nurse visits after Pete had come around a few nights ago.

Pete was watching me, and I smiled back. "I've been remembering more stuff. The day after your accident when you mixed pills and passed out on your bed."

"Well, good morning to you too." I gave Pete a kiss and let him continue.

"Before EG called, I was cleaning the kitchen counter. Like really cleaning. I dropped the toaster, and the bottom tray opened up. Five years of toaster crumbs went flying everywhere. I moved the canisters for the flour, sugar, and stuff, and I found one of your pills. You didn't mix up or combine pills that day. I think you were drugged. You wouldn't climb the stairs to go to bed, if anything you would have gone to the porch. Someone put you there."

"That make sense. That is scarier. Maybe you guys were right, and we should have called the police right away."

"EG gave you something wonderful. I get that, but this cranks it up a whole new level. I know EG said Patty when I mentioned our little issue. Still nothing more from her? EG is on her way here?"

"As far as I know. She hasn't answered any of my texts. I didn't want to go to crazy tracking her down. How do we go from here? The police are looking at you for the fire at the hardware store. Phil is claiming you came charging in there yelling about Patty running me off the road. I know you didn't start the fire, but if we came back with this information, it is not going to look good although hiding it is not good either. There is no way to prove I was drugged."

Pete closed his eyes when he shifted in bed, and I suddenly remembered his locker at Draw Bar with the weed, cash, and switchblade. "Your locker. Speaking of drugs . . ."

286

"I am hoping the drugs are for Pete," my dad said.

"Hey, what are you doing here so early?" I asked

"We got in last night. I dropped your mom off at Peach's. She is meeting Don to review the paperwork for the marriage license. Here are some clothes Sherrie packed for you. There are a couple of pastry bags from Freddie at the nurses station. I'd hurry up. They may not last long. Go eat so I can get some time with my son-in-law."

Pete squeezed my hand. "Go eat. When Jordan comes around, give him the cash. The rest of the stuff is mine."

I kept my face frozen in front my dad. What did Pete just say? The weed and switchblade are his? That is a hell of a secret. Can't count that one as a fun surprise.

It was the first time I was really irked at something Pete had done. This was way bigger than taking off your socks in bed and leaving four pairs stewing at the bottom of the bed for days.

Are there more secrets to this man?

CHAPTER FORTY–SEVEN

A short while later, I was chatting with the nurses, eating a way too sugary pastry and drinking semi-warm coffee when Peggy came off the elevator with a pleasant smile and her tote bag of knitting materials with the reverend following her.

Switchblades and someone else's doctrine is too much for a Saturday morning.

I thought I should give Pete a quick heads-up his mother was gently imposing her will on our wedding, but he would quickly figure it out and there was no stalling her at this point. I greeted them and stayed behind to finish the pastry.

A few minutes later, my dad came out of the room and motioned for me to come. He whispered, "It's ok to do whatever YOU want."

I walked in, hearing Peggy stating her case. "The hospital is obviously fine, but please let him perform the ceremony. If not, then why else did you request Reverend Michael come here?"

"So he can tell you it's ok for Claudia's pastor to perform the ceremony." Pete looked at me and winked. "Now, we would appreciate some time with Reverend Mike here."

That was something else I would not have expected out of Pete. It actually took me seven seconds to respond. His eyes were big and pleading. "Peggy, there is still some mini lemon blueberry scones left that I know you like. Please enjoy them while the three of us talk."

She graciously left us with the reverend only with the prospect of us receiving the gospel.

"Claudia, we haven't meet. I am Reverend Michael from St. Matthews." He extended his hand. We all laughed when I got powdered sugar on his sleeve. He continued, "The first time we are meeting, and I have to start with an apology to you and your friend."

"Ok." That was the most brilliant answer I had.

"C, come here," Pete said. He took my hand, and I sat on the edge of bed. The color in Pete's face was pale and he was sweaty, but he had a shit-ass grin across his face. "Rev, you better explain why."

The mild mannered sixty-year-old man stood there in a gray button-down dress shirt with his hands clasped together almost like he was praying. "Of course. The snowball effect: one mistake and I keep it rolling. I should never have sent that young man to your house or Ms. Minters house without first explaining the situation. To be honest, I thought Pete would have explained our deal, but even if he had, I understand randomly sending a teenage boy to work in your yard should come with a phone call first.

"I was so delighted Pete reached out. I thought it was good idea, and maybe we could do more of this in the future. Especially Jordan seems to be making the most of it. Like most kids, he just needs some direction, and if they don't get it at home, it can lead to some troubling behavior."

"Remember when I told you I started the mentorship program?" Pete asked.

"Last month, you mentioned something about a new program, but I assumed it was at the high school. That is all you said because we were interrupted when some player with the Bucks hit the three-point shot to tie it up."

The reverend jumped in, "A month ago. Down by ten and to come back like that all in the last two minutes."

Pete was about to say something, but I jumped in, "Stay on track please. You two can rehash the game later."

"I totally thought I told you. Nice memory remembering that game when I can't remember last week. Last month, I was working at Draw Bar, taking out the trash in the alley. This kid Jordan is there trying to sell some weed. He is the kid brother to someone I know so I recognized him. I also know he'd been in trouble before. The other kid took off. I confiscated the weed, knife, and money. Told him if he wants his money back, he has work it off and see the Reverend twice a week. If I catch word of him still dealing, all this information goes to the police along with all the surveillance tapes from the alley.

"I called Reverend Mike up and told him I was sending Jordan over to him."

"It was exciting to help our youth and have Pete involved in the church again."

Pete rolled his eyes and let the reverend continue none the wiser that was the only involvement Pete was willing to do with the church. "Fortunately, we have a strong group of ladies that keep our church clean. There is only so much work I can offer a teenager. No snow to shovel and too early to cut the grass. I know better than just to read lessons from the Bible. Pete suggested I have him be in charge of a basketball or kickball game with the kids youth program on Tuesday nights. Give him some responsibility. He has seemed to really take to that. He was anxious for more work. He needed the money so I sent him to do yard work at several houses. It never dawned on me about giving out your address and sending someone unannounced."

"That is ok, reverend. All is forgiven," Pete said, and we laughed at his role of spiritual guider in the room.

"I will pass on your apology to Sherrie," I said.

"Thank you for coming out on such short notice. We appreciate it," Pete said. "Can you spend a few more minutes with my mom, but not too many. I have a feeling C wants to have a few words with me about her finding all that stuff in my locker."

The reverend left the room, and before the door shut, I said, "You really didn't have bring him in here. I would have believed whatever story you told me."

"Good to know. From now on, I'll only have surprises for you. No more secrets, but to be fair, I wasn't not telling you."

"I am angry at myself. Never really thought you were a drug dealer, but I haven't been thinking straight with what we found and then unfound in the basement, my accident, and the fire."

"Shit, that list is getting long. I want to make a funny joke about what you must have thought, but I am too tired to come up with anything," Pete said.

"What do you want me to do with the rest of the stuff?" I asked.

"Where is it?"

"Jorge's garage."

Pete's eyes got big. "I didn't know what to do. You were being questioned about the incident at the hardware store. I didn't want that stuff in the house. Unless Jorge found it and had a little party, it should be all there."

"I hate that this gave you trouble."

"You were doing a good thing. As always, taking care of someone that just needed a push in the right direction . . ." I stopped talking. I couldn't articulate what might not happen such as Pete getting out of the hospital and becoming the best damn school counselor.

Pete let me blow my nose before he said, "That's a pretty good knife. Someone could use it on the boat to gut the fish. I dumped all the ecstasy and left that out of the conversation with the Reverend Mike. If you can do it without a commotion, I am sure Money-Hungry-Jacob would appreciate a bag. Just dump the rest in the river. Give the cash to Reverend Mike and he can give it to Jordan."

"Minus what Sherrie gave him," I said. After I got done telling Pete about Sherrie's naked run through he house, he was ready to sleep again but that would have to wait.

"No, you may not visit my son!" We heard Peggy snap at someone when the nurse opened the door.

Pete and I looked at each other, baffled.

He said, "I haven't heard my mother's voice like that since Marcus drove his four-wheeler through her vegetable garden five years ago."

"Don't make me go out there alone." I laughed.

"Never," Pete said.

The nursed moved to the chair by the window and said, "Don't worry. It's family only in here."

"Any idea who was out there?" I asked.

The nurse was changing Pete's bandages while she spoke, "Lady between sixty-five and eighty-five. Shorter than me and skinny as a rail. She said something about meeting EG."

Pete and I mouthed "Patty?"

"Oh my, you are a Graham. I saw the name Middleton on the visitor log. Thought you looked familiar. Why don't you go settle everyone down out there? We are just going to run some tests and make sure this one gets some sleep."

I was mad at myself for not homing in on the word *tests*. What tests and why. In the end, it wouldn't matter, and maybe for a few hours, I had some joy. I guessed they had run so many tests, drawn his blood, and tested his urine so much, what was one more test? The doctor was worried about something he couldn't pin down.

Patty was gone by the time I got there. My dad had sent her on her way when he reread a text EG had sent her. Patty was insisting she was asked to meet EG here. My dad explained the text meant EG would let her know in two hours when to meet and not to meet in a two hours.

He sent me home to a wonderful surprise. My mom, Mia, Jenna, Kay, and of course Sherrie were there, along with a lady named Jody.

The living room was filled with balloons and cheers when I walked in. My mom explained this was a combination bachelorette party with a mini spa day, dress fitting, and cake tasting.

Jody set up shop in the kitchen, giving each of us a manicure. Mia suggested I try on the dresses before I gorge on cake. Sherrie gave me a pleading look for an explanation when my mom said we should wait to try on dresses for EG to get here. My mom couldn't figure out what was keeping her.

While Jenna popped the champagne, I told Sherrie and my mom about the scene at hospital.

My dad would tell my mom if he hadn't already, and that might explain where EG was but not why?

It felt good to be around all this cheer. I wouldn't let the fact of the rush wedding ruin the afternoon. When my nails were done drying, my mother declared it was time to try on the dresses. My mom did a good job hiding her disappointment about EG being absent.

I was getting more nervous and disappointed. EG has answers, and I wanted them. Was the gift of the house her "get out of jail free" card? She must have known answers were needed, but she didn't seem interested in answering them. Besides answering questions, I realized I didn't need her to physically show up and was teetering on not wanting her to be present for this wonderful afternoon or wedding. I was beginning to understand that no response represented big answers, and she was holding out on me.

Determined not to dwell on the negative, I plunged into trying on dresses. Each dress I tried on had something special about them and each needed some minor alterations. There was not a unanimous vote in the room when my mother said she actually had two more dresses she had brought just for fun. It was her dress and my grandmother's wedding dresses. These semi fit but were not hitting the mark. Sherrie suggested I take the bodice from my mom's dress with the lace Spencer overlay from my grandmother's dress.

Kay, the seamstress of the group, started immediately delicately taking apart the two family dresses for the perfect top. I held up each of the remaining dresses and folded the top down to find the perfect skirt.

Nothing was coming up right when Jody, the outsider of group, suggested the right move. "What about the jeans you have on?" We all turned look at her. "Sorry, didn't mean to intrude. This seems like a nontraditional ceremony. They fit you great, and the blue color is a great match to the vintage lace. Have fun with the shoes. You can go either way with heels or flats."

"That is brilliant," my mother said.

Kay left right after the cake tasting so she could get to work my wedding outfit. I wrapped up the celebration a short time later. I wanted to get back to the hospital. Mia went with Jenna and was going to crash there for the night before heading back the next morning. My mom went to meet my dad somewhere.

I was anxious to get Sherrie alone to explain about Pete's locker and the kid that had showed up. And to get her take on the whole Patty thing showing up at the hospital asking for EG who had yet to show up or answer any texts.

"I wish I had answers for you. This is all so strange. At least your fiancé is not a drug dealer. Not that I ever thought that for one second. We should have known he was doing some greater good for community."

"The unknown questions are digging a hole in my stomach," I said.

"Totally understandable. Want some potatoes to fill that hole?" We laughed, and Sherrie continued, "Are you ok with this wedding? I know it is sweet Pete wanting to put a ring on your finger as fast as he can, but this isn't what you pictured, is it? I know you never wanted the big dress, but you did want to walk down an aisle and have a party."

"I am actually good with this. We can do the big affair later. It may not be what I pictured, but I still get to be married to him."

"That's sweet. To be honest, I am a little sad for me. Not to put it on you, but I was looking forward to a tacky bridesmaid's dress and making faces at you as you walked down the aisle. Now I don't even get to watch."

That all changed a few hours later.

I went back to the hospital. My mom and dad were chatting with Pete's parents. His brother Thomas was in the room. Pete's fever had spiked, and he was fighting some type of infection. It was strictly down to two visitors at a time.

CHAPTER FORTY-EIGHT

EG'S CONTINUING STORY TODAY.

Claudia expected me to answer her texts. My sister expected me to be there. I expected I should be doing something, but I had never prepared for nor could I have even imagined this scenario. Hippie-dippy, peace-loving, make-love-not-war women bring me to my knees. I never believed he attacked her in the parking lot. He doesn't fight, he retreats. He was running away. He was a cheating coward that loved me.

Robert knew the truth was coming out. He left my house dark with a for-sale sign in the yard. He wanted it to look like we had left town. At the inn, he talked about us just going on the road for a while. He loved me, but he didn't love himself. He didn't know himself. When he knew I wasn't leaving River Bend, he had no choice but to go. That's why before I answered the door at the inn I pocketed a piece of paper on my bedside table. It was as much a love note as it was a goodbye note.

Patty never said what had happened to her first husband, but I think Robert paid the price for whatever abuse she'd endured. She told us she started volunteering at a women's shelter after she moved out of the shelter. She said helping others leave their abusive partners made her feel safer. I'm just curious to how much she assisted the women at the shelter . . . was it just emotional support or something more? Patty claims she was protecting me, but I think it was saving her younger self.

How can I face my niece? It brought me little consolation when I learned of Pete's heart condition. Doctors said he probably would not have made it past thirty. These days, with all the medical advancements, you don't know what science could have done for him.

The day Duncan departed Guernsey, the hiking ladies, the EARLs arrived. We never got to hike the island, but they gave me strength to come back here. They were right that I should tell Claudia what I knew and get others to make amends for what they did.

I arrived in the States on Friday and finally found myself in River Bend on Saturday in plenty of the time for the mini pre-wedding celebration but couldn't bring myself to attend. Later that night, I parked my rental car several streets over and walked to the house. From the side window, I saw my sister and Matthew standing in the living room, and again, I couldn't go inside. It was no longer mine.

My old neighbor Jorge had texted me. Asking if he could do anything to help at the house. Claudia, Pete, or Sherrie may have gone to him for help, or he may have heard their scream when the bones were uncovered. I didn't have any answer for him.

I realized I just referred to Jorge my friend as my *old* neighbor.

Weeks ago, I left River Bend not expecting to be back anytime soon. I stood outside of my old home in the dark watching the bedsheets hanging in the porch sway with the wind and thought about what was the basement. How could she do that? It was kinda ingenious and appalling at the same time.

CHAPTER FORTY—NINE

PETE'S LAST DAYS.

Before sunrise Monday morning, we gathered in the hospital chapel. My mom and brother stood up front across from Pete in a wheelchair. Behind him stood his brothers, and his parents sat in the front pew. There was not enough time for Kay to get my wedding ensemble sewn together so I happily wore my Duke sweatshirt as my dad walked me down the four-pew aisle. He kissed my cheek before he turned me to Pete. My dad took my mother's hand, and together, they sat in the front pew.

This was against doctor's orders. Pete should not have been out of bed or his room much less in a wheelchair with ten other people in a room. Our sweet night nurse did not approve either, but for some reason, she pointed out the chapel doors were never locked and a wheelchair sat outside his room.

Rachel, Tommy's wife, had gone in at five a.m., placed her phone in the corner, and set it to record the ceremony. The video I only learned of years later. She said she knew no one would have a steady hand to record the ceremony and thought I might want the video but didn't want to interfere with the special moment. There was eighty minutes of an empty chapel and ten minutes that is forever with me.

Sherrie never got her wish of a tacky bridesmaid dress, but she had the best view of me walking down the aisle when she stood front center as our officiant. Her words were beautiful, personal, and spiritual. She even tossed in two Bible passages my pastor had given her before she entered the chapel. Later, she would say it was to appease Peggy, but deep down I knew she believed in a greater being. I even recited those words at the funeral.

CHAPTER FIFTY

SEVENTY-TWO HOURS AFTER MY WEDDING.

After the fire at the hardware store, so many test were ran on Pete. In addition to the burns, broken ribs and ankle, we learned he had an undiagnosed heart condition. Doctors were so focused on his heart, they missed a bowel injury that lead to sepsis from which he did not recover. On Tuesday morning, they preformed a surgery, but the prognosis was not good. Thursday morning, Pete died while I held his hands.

CHAPTER FIFTY-ONE

EG's Last Story.

Sherrie let me know Claudia was moving off the the patio. She was due back to work full-time next week, and we needed to have answers.

I couldn't remember the last time someone had come after me like Sherrie did. I was staying with my friend Abigail at her condo on the hill overlooking River Bend. Sherrie texted she was on her way without asking if I was there. We barely exchanged hellos when she asked Abigail if we could be alone. Abigail excused herself.

The front door was hardly closed when Sherrie launched into a tirade about being there for Claudia. "You need to come forward now."

I was so startled at how straightforward she was that I instantly put up a wall. "What makes you think I know something?"

"If there was nothing to share, you would not have waited so long to come back here. A phone call is easy to do from anywhere in the world when all you have to say is you don't know anything," Sherrie said.

I nodded and let her continue.

"This isn't a decades-old secret. This is something happening NOW. If you know something, anything, gift or no gift of the house, you must say something, say anything! Someone came after her. We believed she was drugged."

"What do you mean drugged?"

"Jorge and Claudia saw the bones, and a few hours later, she wakes up in her room with no memory of going upstairs. If she were to have moved off the couch, it would have been to the toilet, fridge, or patio, but not upstairs. Pete found the missing pills. Claud didn't mix up her medicine. Even if she wasn't drugged, someone came into the house, sprinkled lye over the body and poured concrete. Someone is hiding a secret."

"Why didn't you call the police?" I asked Sherrie.

"You don't get it. Claud was protecting you. Pete wanted to as did I, but Claud wanted to talk to you first. She had no idea who knew about what was in the basement nor how long it had been there, but her first thoughts were about protecting you. You can leave River Bend, but you can't leave Claudia!"

CHAPTER FIFTY-TWO

Back to Claudia's story and the answers in Madison.

I opened the envelope the man handed me. "Surprise" in Pete's handwriting was written on one side, and the other was "Not a secret but surprise, Love Pete."

The lady from Smith & Madison Title company was gone, and the gentleman told me to follow him to his office. I walked down the hallway, and a door opened. I glimpsed at an NFL quarterback with a contract larger than the state's budget sitting at a table. The baseball hat, sunglasses, and frayed jeans did nothing to hide his identity. Then, if this day couldn't get stranger, when I walked into the man's office Don, Pete's dad, was there.

"Have a seat, Ms. Middleton," the man said.

"Claudia, please call me Claudia. You were at the funeral, but you never came forward," I said.

The man nodded. "Yes, I broke protocol, but I respected Mr. Morris and I wanted to pay my respects."

"Protocol?"

"Yes. Mr. Morris is a client. The one thing we pride ourselves in is privacy and discretion about our services."

"Client?" I looked at Don and the gentleman.

The gentleman answered, "My name is Gerald Landin, and this company is Smith & Madison Title Company and Advisors, LLC."

I looked at Don again, and he spoke for the first time, "There is a lot for you to understand here. We will do our best to explain it all." Don teared up. "Pete loved you so much. We talked about telling you. He struggled so much when it first happened. It took him some time to understand what it all meant and what he wanted out of life. Really wanted. He went on a journey and came out with a pretty good understanding of it all. Mr. Landin and the team here helped with the process."

Don got up from the chair and walked to the window before he started explaining, "It all started on that spring break trip Pete and his buddies took to Florida. They planned to make the drive home in one day like they did going down there. At the last minute, they decided to spend the night outside Atlanta because the rain was so bad."

"I heard this story. No one had any money left, and they all six crashed in one room. The next morning, Pete's car wouldn't start. Pete told the others to pile into Trager's car while he stayed to get his car fixed."

"That is a story the boys love telling." Don and I smiled at the memory we had both shared being in the company of Pete and friends when they talked about that trip. Don and I could both could probably retell the story of when they went deep-sea fishing, and two of them spent more time being seasick than fishing.

Don continued, "Something else happened those five don't know about. Pete decided no one should know until he was ready to tell them."

CHAPTER FIFTY–THREE

Hours after Sherrie confronted EG.

I spent Saturday night in the hospital with Pete. He was slept most of late Saturday afternoon, evening, and throughout the night. Sunday morning, when we had a little time to ourselves, he told me to talk to her. He said he had seen her yesterday, which didn't make sense since only family was allowed and no more than two of us at a time in his room.

He said he understood her motivation and I needed to hear the whole story from them. I don't know if I was emotionally stable, levelheaded, or opened-minded enough to hear anything Patty and EG would have had to tell me. He told me I was safe, and that was all that mattered to him.

His temperature ran high, and he spent most of Sunday sleeping as well. If he was awake, he was negotiating with the hospital staff about our wedding. It would not be done in a hospital room, he told them, stating I deserved better especially if I am marrying him.

"I was safe" repeated in my head. When I asked Pete to tell me what he had learned, he would just say, "You have to listen to her. It is not my story to tell."

A few days later, I'd learn I was wrong to assume the "her" Pete was referring to was not EG. I was worried he was getting delusional. Did Patty actually have a valid answer for running me off the road? When I asked how he had learned something new, he would say, "You know it's a long ride to the MRI scanner, an elevator ride and long hallway. If you know, you know, or you know someone who works in the hospital."

There were a few days between Pete's death and the funeral. After Pete's family and I planned the funeral, I spent time on the patio or walking. After one of my walks, Sherrie declared it was time.

"Time for what?" I asked.

"I have been tasked with getting you answers. Please don't fight me on this. You and I don't have the strength for lengthy battle of wits so just come with me."

Sherrie headed out of town and there were only a few options as to where she was going.

"Are we headed to Aaron's?" My mind spun.

She laughed. "Ah, no. You should see the look on your face trying to connect the dots. Who has the property next door?"

"Molly. Mallory's aunt and uncle," I said.

"Again, since I know you have a lot on your mind, I am just going to give you this one. Don't want you think I am making you walk into an ambush. I heard some of the story, and I think you need to hear the rest of it," Sherrie said.

Before she finished, I said, "Molly is Patty's sister. The lady that drove me off the road and EG's old neighbor so I should be prepared for anything."

"That is probably a good idea," Sherrie answered.

We drove down the long dirt and gravel driveway, and I saw a rental car parked near the door. I turned to Sherrie, "If are doing that thing of no arguing, then let's just assume you know you are coming in and staying with me," I said.

"No shit. I am not missing this. I ain't no Robin to your Batman, no Wonder Girl to your Wonder Woman, only to be pushed out of the big finale." I rolled my eyes and Sherrie spoke again, "Just trying to lighten a tense moment here."

"That's odd, I always thought you were the superhero and I the sidekick," I said.

The side door opened when we approached. EG stepped out and gave me a hug, grabbed Sherrie's hand, and guided us inside. At the kitchen table sat Patty and Molly. In the center of the table was a teapot, some empty mugs, and baked goods. My first thought was *What's with old people and their tea?*

Sherrie and I sat side by side, with EG to my left, Patty across from us, and Molly to the right.

Patty spoke first. "Thank you for coming."

I was not in the mood for small talk, and neither was anyone else. Molly offered us tea, but we declined.

EG led the conversation. "When I am stuck with my writing, I tell myself to stop overcomplicating things and just start. A beginning is just a beginning, and I can also add to it later. We owe you the whole story."

"We." EG knew! *"We owe you the whole story."* I couldn't believe it. Then I remembered Pete was ok with it so I think I needed to hear them out before I passed judgment. I was having Chuck watch the house because of these old ladies?

Molly didn't add anything until the end. Together, the two of them, EG and Patty, the former professor, told me the story.

EG said she was not sure if she was more shocked at Robert's death or that he was Robert. Throughout the story, Patty was stoic but broke down towards the end.

"I was married before I met Phil. My first husband, Eddie, was wonderful and charismatic when he wanted to be. My mother did not want us to get married. I thought I knew better. Eddie and I ran off together. Things changed quickly, but I stayed because I couldn't go home after the things I said to my mother. I was too stubborn to admit she was right and there were times it was good. Some days, he was the man I loved, and other days I didn't know who he was."

Patty stopped talking. Her hand shook but not other signs of emotion showed when she paused to sip some tea.

Molly said, "He can't hurt you now."

Patty put down the tea and turned her forearm towards me and Sherrie and said, "I got this scar one night from his belt because . . ."

Molly stopped her. "You don't need to tell us."

"I just want the girls to understand my experience and to know I would never let another woman go through what I did. I'd seen the same signs in Duncan, well, Robert as he was. After you go through what I did, you see people differently and pick on things. My fear increased when I first spoke to his brother, but it wasn't until we connected in person that night that I . . . that I knew I had to confront him.

"The night of the storm, I was ashamed of myself for letting EG leave with him. Robert was on such a high, I knew at some point he would snap. It could be days or weeks, but I knew he was freight train ready to go off the rails.

"I thought at first I did the right thing telling them to take the truck as if that would keep EG safe. An hour later, Duncan—the real Duncan—showed up, and we talked. He told me how unstable Robert is. I was scared I pushed too hard exposing his cheating and plagiarism.

"Phil had fallen asleep in his chair. I called Molly, and she picked me up. We'd gone to the inn that night to tell EG what I had learned from the real Duncan and to warn her. The person working there would not tell me what room she was in. Remember, there were no cell phones then. The best I could do was use the inn phone and be connected to the room. Robert answered, and I told him I needed to speak to EG. He said he would have her come down.

"We waited and waited and no sign of either of them. I left Molly watching for EG. I went to the car to wait, and sometime later, he came out with his suitcase. He was going to leave. Runaway. I confronted him in the parking lot. I have to say, I was not in my right mind. He pushed me away. I should have just let him go. He laughed at me and asked how I was going to stop him, and this time, he pushed me into the truck. Two nights prior, EG had come to my house because she knew better and stepped away from the situation when Robert started to lose it. She was didn't say anything, but I know the signs.

"The rain was coming down hard. I was screaming at him, asking if EG was ok. He slapped me. I was so scared I was too late. I needed to stop him. I flung open the tailgate of the truck cab. I had no idea what was in the bed of the truck. Just hoping something from the hardware store would be in there. I wanted to slash the tires. If he left, he would just continue his lie to destroy who knows how many other lives. I had gone to protect EG, but if he left, there would be others. I had not been the first women Eddie treated poorly. For years, I was upset that others had experienced what I did and no one had said anything to me. No one stood up to him. I was mad at the world. It was a miracle I found Phil and could trust someone again."

Patty's emotional brick wall started to crack, wiped her eyes and continued, "Sorry, hon. I know you want the one story. Part of me needs to explain my behavior. It does not excuse it but will maybe help you understand."

All I could do was nod my head.

Patty continued, "In the bed of the truck, I found Phil's toolbox. I grabbed the hammer, and I was going to claw the tire. He got out and tried pushing me away, but my arm was in full motion, and I hit . . . him. I was aiming for the tire. The claw hit him in the knee. He pushed me away, and then he bent down, grabbed his knee, and I was swinging again and knocked him in the head. He swung at me, and I swung the hammer.

"I don't know if I swung more or not. It rocks me to know I had that much evil in me. I was not better than him. I was judge and jury."

Molly spoke next. "I'd come out of the inn at this point being so nervous because I hadn't seen anyone. Robert was on the ground, and I knew. I knew I had to protect my sister. By the grace of god, we found the strength to hoist him into my trunk. It was dark and cold and . . . Sorry, until a few days ago, when we finally told EG what happened, I have never spoken the words so this might be a little blunt."

Patty straightened up. "Oh, get on with it, Molly. At this point, just blurt out that when we slammed the trunk shut, we severed his hand off. Behind the inn were several propane tanks for the outdoor grill. I threw two of them in truck, and Molly followed in her car. We went to the bend in that road, and I got out let the truck roll. I tossed the hand."

"Molly drove me home, and I waited for the police to show up when they identified the truck.

"I am not proud nor am I ashamed of what I did that night, but the next day I was wrecked with guilt. EG married this man, and I took him away. Maybe that wasn't my choice. Robert paid for the mistakes my Eddie made.

"I thought about telling EG but didn't know how she would react, so I did what I thought would give me insurance if she didn't believe I had done it for her best interest. My insurance plan was putting the evidence in her house. I wasn't sure if they would see the damage to skull if we put Robert in the truck before we pushed it over the hill. That could come back to EG. Who else could have done that to Robert? I just had to make sure there was an explosion to possibly cover up the lack of a body. Whatever the police found or did not find EG, lost her husband that night."

Patty chuckled and continued, "That Monday, the detective came over to tell EG that besides the hand, there was little DNA at the scene. She was telling us too much, but we weren't stopping her. She did not think foul play was involved but didn't know if they could rule Duncan dead.

"At one point, when they came to ask more questions, I had Phil start to remove that tank. Just a neighbor helping another neighbor. He had removed the top half of the tank from the steel legs and put it in the corner. Phil was jackhammering the floor to remove the base when they came down to ask him to stop. He even asked the one detective to help carry the empty drum upstairs. The men determined it was too wide and may have to stay were it was. The house may have been built around it. I remember laughing when the detective offered advice on that quick-pour cement and make sure we read the instructions. Phil answered, 'You do know I own the hardware store.'

"The detective said, 'I drive a car but that doesn't mean I know how it works.'

" 'Fair point. Then come back after your shift. I'd appreciate the help,' Phil said.

" 'How about I just give you a call and read the directions out loud?' "

EG finally spoke up, "I had no reason to doubt that Robert was in the truck. He was never declared dead. I was told I could petition the court to declare him dead or wait seven years. There was nothing for me to gain by declaring him dead. There was no insurance money and more legal trouble considering the university thought he was Duncan. His mother just needed to be told he died, and Duncan took care of that. I held a small memorial service. It was mostly friends of mine, Katie Lyn and Matthew, two of his dorm mates and a few others from his classes. It was more powerful realizing the world was not going to miss him."

Patty spoke, "EG had no idea we put him there a day later. It wasn't until she talked to Pete, and then it was only a guess."

Molly went next. "It was all to protect to EG." She stood up like that was the end of it.

I don't think Sherrie had ever been so fast with a command. "Hell no. Sit down." Even I was scared. "That was fine back then. We get it. Although I can't speak for EG. You three will have to settle that. Now let's not forget the run down and the drugs and what happened in that store."

"Yes, yes, I need to own that too," Patty said. "Phil said that you had started renovations. We had no idea the house was yours. I just wanted to talk to Pete. I saw his truck, and I thought I could wave him down. Most people know what a waving hand means, especially down a country road where you know everyone. I veered to other side thinking we both would stop."

"Are you saying a single female should just pull over on the side of the road? Do you know what type of shit happens out in the world these days?" Sherrie answered.

I didn't reign her back in. Just kept my eyes on Patty.

"Now that you say it like that, I can see my mistake. I think my heart stopped when the truck rolled and to see you in the ditch. Not that it would have made a difference if it was Pete. I just wanted to fix what I did all those years ago. We went to see you, and I thought if we took care of it, I could say it was a neighbor helping a neighbor who was home recouping. I just gave you something to knock you out for a few hours. Still hadn't come up with a story about what was done there. Was hoping to talk to EG and didn't realize she was out of the country.

"Pete came storming into the hardware store. Oh, boy I knew I made a mistake with all of it. I tried calming him down. He was yelling so much the whole store could hear him. He was so scared for you. He pounded his fist on the metal shelf, and some material scattered across the floor. I had to stop him from saying too much, so I caused a bigger commotion and I pushed a shelf over. Something knocked into something else, and before I knew it, the place was on fire. A hardware store with stuff that had been on shelves for years was just kindling waiting for a spark."

"Ok," I said. From corner of my eye, I could see Sherrie looking at me for the rest of my answer, but that was it. People are still lying and covering for each other, but at least I knew Sherrie got all this recorded on her phone.

After a minute, I finally said to Patty and Molly, "Can you give us a minute?" Normally that would call for them to leave the room, but I asked EG and Sherrie to follow me outside. I needed some fresh air in order to keep going.

We walked to an old picnic table on the back side of the house and sat down. Sherrie slid in next to me, almost missing the seat. I think for the first time in a long time I was more steady than her.

I didn't know why my mind was wandering to Duncan. "The real Duncan. "What does he know?"

"He believes Robert died taking that curve too fast in the ice storm. As did I until a few days ago. He actually believed trying to declare Robert dead would be difficult with no benefit. He could also control the narrative for his mother. She was in a delicate state mentally and physically. After a few months, he gathered up some wood ash and bought an urn and told his mother Robert died. A few weeks later, she passed from lung cancer. I connected with him eight months after Robert died when I traveled to London."

Sherrie and I exchanged looks.

I said, "What aren't you saying?"

"Don't worry, I am not holding anything back." EG looked like her mind was a thousand miles away. "We have been meeting up for years. Sometimes, we see each other twice a year or go two years without seeing one another. Very little communication when we are apart. We really only

327

communicate to arrange our next trip together, or it is strictly business. We know we could never be together as a couple. For so many reasons, his career being one and the other is the ghost of his brother.

"I never had this raw chemistry with any other man as I do with him. It is strange, wild, and probably sharing too much, but at this point I don't know if it matters. Physically and sexually, he is truly unmatched to anyone I have ever met. This arrangement has worked out well for us.

"I don't know if it is out of some association guilt for Robert's deception or if he just really wanted to get his work published, but all the books I write under the pen name Mo Robert Earl is mostly Duncan's work. It is the young adult novels. Duncan and I have a contract with me getting the majority of the royalties. And that book series really pays well.

"Mo came from their surname Morgan, and we decided to use Robert's name for him to sadly or weirdly get some published writing credit posthumously. I told Duncan that Earl is just a random name, but it from the best group of ladies I knew back then and still to this day . . . Earl is from my hiking group, EG, Arlene, Rhonda, and Lydia.

"In a way, all three are why I never needed a traditional marriage. Although technically Duncan and I are still married. Robert scared me from really trusting another man again. I get the best sex of my life when Duncan and I connect. And the ladies of EARL are my spirit and deepest friendships."

PART 3

THE END

CHAPTER FIFTY–FOUR

Claudia's story continues in Mr. Landin's office.

Don said, "Pete does have a letter for you explaining all of this, but he preferred I tell you the story. He figured you would start crying and not be able to read the letter. There are two letters actually to be read later. I don't know what's in them. Pete wrote them and sealed the envelopes. I know one was written before the engagement. Mr. Landin will give them to you later. May I suggest you read them much later. Let all this sink in first.

"There is a lot to unfold here, so let me get straight into it. That spring break trip to Florida happened exactly as told. Same for the ride north in the torrential downpour that forced them into some roadside motel. After a ten-minute cutthroat game of rock-paper-scissors, Pete lost, which had him going in the rain to the liquor store for beer.

"While he was there, he bought himself a lottery ticket. The next morning, they are at Waffle House. He goes to the bathroom, and some girls in line say someone local won the lottery last night. Yes, in the bathroom at Waffle House, Pete looks up the numbers and knows he won. He knows his life is about to change. He heads back to the table and sees all the guys laughing and talking. Trager was laughing so hard he was crying. One of the guys was so broke he was counting quarters trying to decided if he could afford the two meat breakfast platter when a quarter rolled off the table. Pete thought he could buy everyone in the place the two-meat breakfast platter and probably buy the entire restaurant. Instead of saying something, he froze. He wants to tell them, obviously, but he knew everything would change. He may never have a moment like this again with these friends. Friends that are friends because of who they are.

"He sat down and immediately got back up and went to bathroom and threw up.

"He does something I don't think I could have done. He keeps it quiet. When they are packing up to leave the motel that morning, he tells them his car won't start. He tells them all to go on without him. Somebody wants to stay, but he insists they all leave and says something about getting a part for the car. Pete calls and gives me the same story but wants me to fly down.

"He picks me up at the airport, and we go out to dinner. I think he is losing his mind because he acting so odd. Giddy and won't completely answer one question until we are at dinner at Atlanta's most expensive restaurant. At this point, I was thinking he was doing some type of drugs during spring break that was causing this maniac behavior I had never seen before in him.

"When I refused to have a sip of the most expensive wine in the restaurant, he finally told me.

"We decided the best thing to do was to do nothing. He had one-hundred-eighty days to claim the winnings. I tried to get him to see a psychologist, but he wouldn't. I told him after high school I hitchhiked to California and spent a year being a beach bum and surfer. I realized after a year I wanted to come back and raise my family here. I suggested the same thing to Pete."

"Surf?" I said.

Don and Mr. Landin both laughed. Don kept going, "Travel. Go travel and it will either land you somewhere else, or you know you want to come back. He didn't take me up on it initially, and then finally he went."

"The Europe trip," I said.

"In Atlanta, you don't have to publicly announce you are the winner. After some research and talking to the right folks, I found Mr. Landin. We will get back to him in a minute.

"So finally Pete went. He would call occasionally. His mother hadn't ever traveled outside of the States and was so worried about him. The one thing Pete asked of me was never to tell anyone. Including his mother. It was a hard conversation. To this day, I struggle with it. I understand his choice, but it doesn't make it easy for me. However, now that he is gone, I like that I have a piece of him that I don't need to share with anyone.

"Back to the trip. Trager joined him for the first ten days. Four months after Trager returned, Pete seemed a little different on the phone. Something was off. I can't describe it. I had a passport from our fishing trips to Canada so I decided to join him. Peggy was relieved.

"When I got there, he had been volunteering at the orphanage for a week. I thought I would find him happy with all the hands-on work he was doing. The first time I saw his face, I barely recognized him. He was working nonstop. Repairing walls, building a play area, painting, repairing the roof, on and on. It was guilt driving this work. How could these children live in such a

336

godforsaken place, and he, who didn't really need much, was gifted something so enormous.

"He couldn't sleep, and I don't know if he was eating. At this point, we had made initial contact with Mr. Landin. Smith & Madison Title Company are financial advisors and more. Much more. They are not the kind that recommend a good 401K and make it possible to retire two years early. When Pete claimed the winning lottery numbers, Mr. Landin set up the right accounts and kept it as private as possible. I remember Mr. Landin said they had other services available, and I dug into that.

"Together, we convinced Pete to talk to someone. Mr. Landin sent someone. For three days in that tiny village, they talked. Pete came out if it with acceptance and an understanding of his situation. It was that old adage you can give a fish to a man and he eats for a day or you teach him how to fish and he can eat for a lifetime. This is silly to say it this way, but Pete learned he could eat, give others fish to eat, and teach others to fish. One does not have to affect the other one.

"With Mr. Landin's team, Pete set up a charitable organization. Pete knew he couldn't cure the world of hunger or single-handedly save a village. He needed to live his life. He most certainly wanted to remain anonymous. He would pick several charities a month to receive donations. Mr.

Landin would vet them and decide who gets the money. Pete loved this as he didn't want a god complex. He didn't know if he was personally saving the Michigan coastline or buying the new van for the food bank. If he selected three charities that month, he wouldn't know if one or two got the money. All the spending is well documented and within IRS guidelines."

"The money the boys get each year. The ten thousand dollars is not from you," I said.

Don nodded. "He wanted to do something with the money for his mom and me and his brothers. I always handled the finances. The selling of the condo in Florida at the right time was a great cover story.

"Back to that tiny village, after the those days with the counselor, Pete felt better. He set up an endowment for the place to receive help each year. After that, we headed to northern Italy and had some of the best food and wine I ever had in my life. We took a three-day luxury cruise to Greece. Pete may have known how to help people, but he also knew he could enjoy things. That is the second secret I kept from Peggy. We told her we were still in that village and not living it up on a cruise. We still laugh about it these days. I told him I had to fatten him back up before he saw his mother again, or she would be mad at me."

"The one thing I saw was no matter how much fun and food we were having, he was missing something. It was a several years ago he found it. When he met you. A few years ago during that ugly incident at the bar when he was shot and when he knew he would be fine, he couldn't stop talking about you and your bravery and refusing to leave his side when all hell was breaking out. I didn't know you at the time. We were still in Florida then. I told him he should ask you out, and then he let me know hitting on his boss's girlfriend was not cool. As far I know, he went on a few dates with others, nothing serious with anyone. I knew there was something special about the one he couldn't ask out."

Tears dropped from my eyes. Mr. Landin placed a tissue in my hand and took the water glass I didn't know I was holding.

"Did Pete give you the whole secrets versus surprise manta?" Don asked.

"Over and over again."

Don answered, "That was more for his mental well-being than anything else. Now, that brings us to the next portion of this visit."

"Ok," I said.

Mr. Landin spoke but twisted his pitch to sound like Pete. "Surprise." Don and Mr. Landin shared a laugh before Mr. Landin continued, "As his wife and even without the marriage, Pete instructed you to be the solo beneficiary of his estate minus the modest sum for his brothers and parents."

"Me?"

Mr. Landin looked at Don, and Don said to him, "You know you have to say. Pete said and to quote my son, 'I'll haunt your ass if you don't follow my instructions.' So start over. And, Claudia, say that line again just like you did. Pete figured it would go down this way, and he has a tremendous sense of humor and very strict step-by-instructions."

Mr. Landin repeated those bold words, "As his wife and even without the marriage, Pete instructed you to be the solo beneficiary of his estate minus the modest sum for his brothers and parents."

Don looked at me, and I said again, "Me?"

Mr. Landin said, "Yeah, you." Then he pressed a button on a remote, and music filled the room. The '80s song, "Wish You Were Here" by the Thompson Twins from the movie *Sixteen Candles* came on. In the movie, the song begins playing during the romantic climax when Samantha and Jake are sitting on the dining room table. My father had given me his love of '80s music and my mother '80s movies.

Posthumously Pete recreated one of my favorite romantic movie scenes. I didn't know if I had more tears or laughter streaming from me. I loved that man. Even in death, he could bring me joy. Playing an '80s tune hit me in my soul. I would forever miss and love him.

"Excuse me for a moment," Mr. Landin said, and he left Don and me for a bit. Shock was overwhelming. I asked more about the Europe trip. Don walked around the room while he spoke. He lit up when telling those stories. He and I stood in front of the windows behind Mr. Landin's desk.

I asked, "The fishing trips to Madison?"

"We did get some fishing in but mostly a cover story for when we met with Mr. Landin and his team." We all turned when the office door open. Mr. Landin and another gentleman walked in.

"Speaking of team, I would like to finally introduce myself. I am Cade Whitmore." He extended his hand, and I was slow to meet it.

I finally took his hand and said, "Claudia, Nice to finally meet you. Do we know each other? You look familiar."

"We have not met, but you have seen me twice. Please have a seat, and we can explain." He pointed to the sofa to the left of Mr. Landin's desk. Don and I took a seat, and he and Mr. Landin pulled the chairs Don and I had just been in to face us.

Cade spoke, "I was trying to find a moment to speak to you. Someone is always with you. You are very fortunate. We see many people with such great wealth, and they are the loneliest and therefore some of the most miserable people. I tried to find you while you were on one of your walks. I didn't want to scare you, and when I was finally in a space I could approach, you deviated from the path."

"You were the runner." He nodded, and I kept talking. "You kept good form going up the hill. But how in the hell you were going to approach me along a deserted part of the trail without me going postal."

"I saw the bear spray handing from your wrist. Trust me, I was aware. I was hoping Don would have given you some type of heads-up about us. Without that, the only thing we have is the code word that Pete said we could use: Ben Butler."

I responded, "This was better to meet you now. Even hearing those words I would've released the bear spray."

"I guess I made the right decision."

"And the second time? When did we see each other?" I asked.

"In the stairwell at the hospital."

"You are the one that gave me the tissues."

"Yes. Pete—well, Don had reached out the night prior," Cade said.

Don spoke next, "Pete was conscious the evening prior for a bit. You had gone to dinner with friends, and Peggy stepped out. Pete told me the plan for the wedding and asked me figure out how to get a license fast and to—"

"To keep it a surprise," I said.

"Now you are sounding like him," Don said. "By the way, I don't feel bad for keeping those few minutes I has with him alone a secret. Peggy doesn't even know. Married for decades and these are the only two secrets between us."

I turned back to Cade. "You were in scrubs. In the stairwell."

"It is pretty easy getting around a hospital in scrubs. I even got past Cheryl's desk a few times."

"I had someone watching the house during the funeral. I had seen you somewhere else, and someone was asking about me at work. You need to do better." My nerves were making me say whatever came to mind.

"Understood," Cade said. "Your friend Chuck is good. Not our kind of good. We spotted him and held back especially since we figured he was there because either you or your friend Sherrie had spotted us following you. Two days after your accident, Pete had us watching you and the house."

I couldn't help smile. "Of course he did." No wonder he let me handle things so slowly.

Mr. Landin eyed Cade and did not look happy especially since discretion was a primary function of their business.

Mr. Landin spoke next, "We would like to continue to serve you as we did with Pete. We offer many services. Financial, everything from growing your money, investing, philanthropy, and keeping you on the right side of the IRS. Everything we do is legal, but not everything we do is public. We have many, many services we can help you with. We can execute court documents in a very timely manner and remove you from hostile foreign countries. That is not our favorite, but it is something we had to do for some clients. We are typically not seen nor do we want to be. You can see from our storefront or lack thereof."

"The credit card I found with the name Gunner L. Driver. That was set up by you?"

"We do that so there is not an easy trace back to our clients. Pete had us working on a card for you."

"Ah, um, after all I just heard, I am suddenly nervous, What name did he request?"

Mr. Landin actually laughed. "Based on the premise it would draw too much attention, I refused the name of Chunky Monkey."

After I laughed, everyone else in the room did too. Ben and Jerry's ice cream will forever be in my heart and on my hips.

"You can change it to anything you like, but he finally picked, Samantha Turner." I smiled and kept it from the men. I didn't need to share everything with them today. Samantha was Samantha Baker from *Sixteen Candles*, and Turner from the '70s, '80s, and beyond rock icon Tina Turner.

Mr. Landin spoke, "Like I said, we offer a variety of services. Once you sign on to be our client, we will review in further detail what we offer. I will also suggest two other firms that do what we do. They are very good, but I think we offer more. We want you to be comfortable in your decision."

Cade said, "We have given you a lot of information. No decision has to be made today. This is only the first step. We have arranged for some sandwiches and beverages in the boardroom next door for you and Don. We will be right here to answer any questions. Just press the button on the table, and we will come to you.

"I do have to remind you about the sign-in form you filled out with Ms. Jones when you entered our outer office. Even if you choose not to use our services, you are not allowed to talk about this visit or our company. We take our nondisclosure agreements very seriously."

"As you should." That was the only line I could come up with.

Cade walked us to a small boardroom and closed the door. I turned to Don and started about five sentences but never got past, "What . . . How . . . What about . . . Does . . . Umm."

"That pretty much sums it up," Don said. "The only piece of advice I will give you is tell one person. Pete chose me. Honestly, it was a burden at times, but I one hundred percent would not have wanted it another way. I could understand why he was so messed up emotionally. He could buy anything. He also knew he couldn't buy family and friends. Sometimes, I wondered what would have happened if he had discovered the windfall at a different time. He never wanted his relationship with his friends to change. He knew what was important."

"So when he talked about building the dream mountain cabin. He wasn't just dreaming. He was building it," I said.

"The plans were all drawn up. He has the land in Colorado. The plans were changed since you came into the picture, and he added your wish list items. It was going to be a wedding gift of sorts."

"I am nervous to know what he took seriously."

"He was planning on telling you about all this. He just didn't want anything to change."

"I get it," I said. I grabbed a cookie from the lunch platter. It crumbled to pieces. "You would think they could afford better cookies here. So what are we talking about?"

Don answered, "Mr. Landin, or his team, had set up a fake news article including a photo of Pete holding a large cardboard check. The small news article explained him winning the lottery in some state while he was on a fishing trip. The fake check was for three hundred thousand dollars. Smith & Madison Associates do this for some of their clients to explain the sudden change of cash flow."

"I think you are telling me its more than three hundred thousand."

Don didn't answer.

"A million?"

Don still didn't answer.

I drank some water trying to understand what Don was not telling me when he finally said, "They will bring in some paperwork. Again, no decisions need to be made, but you need understand the scope of things. It is a pretty good nest egg."

CHAPTER FIFTY-FIVE

Just after leaving Mr. Landin and Cade.

I was almost to River Bend when I decided that if we are doing this celebration of life to repair our missing hearts, I needed to do one more thing. EG had given me this house and, with that, a piece of this town. It was all a little broken, but I wanted to fix that.

My Jeep kicked up the dirt when I turned into the gravel driveway. I had never been there before and could only guess at the location. The house was set off the road, but the mailbox clearly displayed their names.

I knocked on the door, and no one answered. I hit the doorbell and waited. Wasn't sure what my plan was if they weren't home.

"Didn't expect you. Phil and I are sitting out back," Patty said.

She didn't wait for me to follow. By the time I caught up with them, Patty had taken a seat next to Phil. The Brewers were playing a doubleheader that day. Phil had a beer and peanuts, and the game on. I guessed that's what an owner of a hardware store does on a Saturday when his store is burned down.

I didn't sit and just started, "I know what you did was out of love for EG and maybe payback for what you endured years earlier. It is not for me to judge what happened to Robert. I think I can understand why you never told her. Decisions are made fast especially when you are threatened and you think you are doing it for the right reasons.

"I am not here to forgive you for drugging me, and I'm not naive enough to think you need my forgiveness to move on. You made decisions and have to live with them. I'm giving you honesty here. I am not sure I believe that story about trying to flag down the truck to talk to Pete. We will never know if you ran me off the road thinking you were shutting down or slowing down Pete discovering Robert in our basement. All I know is you put me in jeopardy with your decisions.

"There will be no lawsuits or counter lawsuits for running me off the road or you claiming Pete blew up your store or defamation or anything else. The bullshit stops now.

"Come with me to the bonfire. We are going to show a united front, and let this town come together again. It can work if we are there together."

Phil turned off the radio. He shook my hand. Patty stood and I braced for a hug, but she just nodded and asked, "Peggy and Don ok with us coming?"

I nodded in agreement and said, "They want to move forward too." I was shaking with relief. Then the old hippie and I took each other's words as the finale to all this shit. I knew she was good at keeping secrets. They walked to the Jeep with me.

"When are you going to start the rebuild? Insurance come through yet?" I asked.

Patty said, "Insurance is going to fight it, but everything was to code and the fire chief can't determine it was anything but an accident."

"What are you going to do until then?" I asked

Phil answered, "Retire. I was thinking about it before the accident. I was gonna sell the store. I could have gotten decent money for it. Now, I'll get whatever insurance is willing to pay out."

"He's been talking retirement for years. Never thought it was going to happen. Now he'll have time take care of the to-do list I have had for this house for nineteen years."

I watched Phil hoist Patty up to the front seat of the Jeep, and he climbed in back. "What's first on your list?"

Patty did a double look at me and started giggling. "Finish the basement."

The Jeep roared to life, and we laughed. The drive down the gravel driveway hid my shaky hands, and I had to bite my lip to suppress a big smile. Pete had told me Patty talked to him in the hospital. She had a friend that worked there, and she knew when Pete would be transported to a lower floor for some testing.

She admitted they drugged me and poured lye all over the body. They hadn't intended to do the floor, but I was really out of it and knew I shouldn't be left alone until they thought I would be ok or someone would be home shortly. They saw the ready-quick cement and figured it might deter us from digging up the area again.

Pete had said he admired her honesty. She wasn't there for forgiveness, only to rationalize her actions. I remembered the rest of Pete's words, "Her lack of remorse bothered me. She did all of those things she determined to be ok. It's the world according to Patty, and everyone watch out. Didn't mean to torch the place, but I did set display of sparklers on fire. I swear something else happened but I just can't remember. Maybe tomorrow the memory will come back."

CHAPTER FIFTY-SIX

PATTY'S STORY.

No excuses or further explanation for of my actions. I stand by everything I did to Robert, hiding the evidence, even drugging Claudia, including tossing that can of butane into the cardboard display of sparklers Pete lit on fire.

Molly and I have been getting away with stuff for years. She has more varieties of weed and herbs growing on her land than a farmer in Jamaica. Maybe I didn't need to run Claudia off the road, but how was I to know it her and not Pete.

I had told Phil not to put that sparkler display out so early in the season. He'd saved the unsold stuff from last year in that damp basement storage area under the store. I thought we would get complaints about the dead product. I couldn't be happier to be wrong. I knew it would take something dramatic to get Phil to finally retire.

Claudia is driving down the driveway biting her lip. I hope she is not getting too emotional about going to Pete's celebration of life. I can't handle weak women.

CHAPTER FIFTY–SEVEN

Evening of the bonfire and celebration of life.

There was an audible gasp from the people that saw me, Patty, and Phil emerge from the Jeep. Don and Peggy walked over, and handshakes and hugs were exchanged. Don and I kept our speeches short, and then we quickly lit the bonfire before Marcus could start talking.

Music blared from somewhere, and jello shots were passed around. Jello shots with a basil garnish.

Marcus pulled me aside. I wasn't avoiding him, maybe I was, I just didn't want anything but happiness now. "Claudia, can I have quick second?"

"Now?"

"Please."

"What can I do for you, Marcus?"

He bent over and whispered, "I know."

"Know what?"

"First, I don't want anything. It's all yours. Just don't give me that damn line about surprises."

"What are you talking about?"

"Let me guess, you and my dad went fishing this morning," Marcus said.

I stayed quiet, and I hadn't really had much time to figure anything out.

Marcus kept going. "My parents don't have that kind of money. It took me about a year and a half to figure it out. A little research helps. I don't want any of it, but please keep it going for my brother for another year or two if possible. Not sure how much is left. They are building a house and trying to start a family. Give them my share for the year."

Still hadn't moved a muscle.

"It's ok, relax. At the engagement party, I was all about the prenup because that would typically be me. Thomas is the dutiful eldest son, Pete is the caretaker, and I am the fun, loud one. Please don't tell my dad I know. Let him have this secret with Pete.

"Sorry, if I was being pushy with CiCi the other week. I felt like I was playing the role of the obnoxious brother and didn't know when or how to stop."

"You did a fine job," I said.

Marcus laughed so I laughed at my non-joke.

He said, "I am serious, I don't want anything. Let that be what I got from my brother, looking out for others. I found the article about Pete winning the three hundred thousand dollars."

For years, he and Thomas continued to receive what Pete set aside for them. And maybe a far bit more when Don and Peggy died. Their estate was bigger than Thomas or Marcus had expected it to be. Well, at least Marcus knew where it had come from, even if he thought it was part of the three hundred thousand Pete didn't win.

Maddie and my brother were holding hands as they waited for the keg to be tapped. I spotted my ex Aaron talking to Sherrie. I was happy he was able to celebrate Pete's life with the rest of the town. If I could be friends with my ex, maybe this town could come together. Bringing Patty and Phil here was more for the town than it was for me. I didn't know if, like EG, I could move past everything Patty had done. One day, Patty would have to answer for everything she had done. In no way what I did in a few months compared to what Patty had done. I only kept a great secret. A BIG secret. One day, I will be ready to tell him.

Sherrie bounced over with blue lips from the jello shots. "You look great in your fancy yet causal clambake attire." I was wearing jeans with an antique white lace sleeveless top. I had to wear part of wedding dress at some point. She handed me a jello shot, and I asked, "Who puts a garnish on a jello shot?"

"You won't believe it. Peggy didn't want you thinking she wasn't ok with the party. I guess there was some argument when planning the funeral. She said she Googled what to bring, and somehow jello shots came up in her search. She thought the colorful treats looked fun."

We laughed. I said, "I could use a few more of them."

Sherrie replied, "I could use a few days in Barcelona."

"Let's go."

"Go where?"

"Barcelona, Paris, Rome, or anywhere else," I said with a straight face. "This summer right after your last class."

"You are serious, aren't you?"

"Yup."

"Hell yes. I say Paris. No, Barcelona. No, wait. Let's see where it's cheaper to fly into."

"How about all of them?"

"How about one each summer. I will get a third job. This will be fun."

"My treat."

"You can't be serious."

"This morning's road trip was to see a lawyer about Pete's estate." I don't feel bad for lying to Sherrie now because I told her truth when she gave up her secret while we were in a hospital in Zurich. "Pete's parents gave me everything, the boat, insurance money for the truck, and his annual inheritance payout."

"You can't be serious," Sherrie repeated.

"Maddie!" I screamed, and she came running over. "I think we found a place for you this summer. Rent-free. Do you mind housesitting?"

"I would love to!" Maddie yelled.

"So you will go with me?" I asked Sherrie.

"A hundred percent!" she said.

"How about a two-hundred twenty-nine million percent," I said. She missed the tear from my eye when she hugged me. That's right, Pete did not win a little lottery, he had won the Powerball. All two-hundred-twenty-nine million dollars.

CHAPTER FIFTY-EIGHT

SHERRIE'S STORY.

I never found the great love of my life, but I had a great life and great love and that is all you need. That, and a friend like Claudia.

We hit Europe running. We landed and stayed in Paris for a few days and then took the train south and meandered over to Italy and then headed to Romania.

Rome and Venice slowed us down. I was tired. Claudia was fidgety. The whole trip her leg never stopped bouncing. I never said anything because it was so good to see her moving around and off the porch. She was putting one foot in front of the other, maybe running away from the sadness, but at least she was moving forward. Not moving on but moving forward.

One afternoon after arriving at that little inn in the village in Romania, we finally snapped at each other.

"What's your problem?" Claudia asked.

"You won't sit still," I said. "And this trip is amazing but seriously, we have to be running low on the Pete fund. I feel like I am sponging off you. With probably the exception to this dump, we have been staying at some nice, I mean really nice, hotels and AirBnbs. You said it was all a gift, but come on now."

"I will explain when you tell me why you skipped that gondola ride. I felt silly by myself. Do you know the comments I got from the obnoxious tourists watching. 'Hey, lady, this isn't a single's cruise. Hey, missy, the boats are wide enough for two.' The pitying looks from those standing on the bridges was a bit much for me. You talked about it for three weeks and suddenly just bailed."

"You didn't have to go. I will give you the money for it," I said.

"It's not about the money. What's wrong?"Claudia demanded.

"I didn't think I should step on a small boat. I've been dizzy. Really dizzy. Three months ago, I didn't hit a pothole on my bike. I just fell over and tweaked my wrist. At the Vatican, I didn't get separated because I followed a hot guy on a different tour. I was so nauseous I spent thirty minutes on the nicest marble bathroom floor I had ever seen before I was escorted out."

"Oh shit!" Claudia said.

"And I think . . ." The room went blurry and then dark.

CHAPTER FIFTY—NINE

SHERRIE'S STORY CONTINUED.

I immediately knew I was in a hospital bed when I woke up. There was an IV taped to my hand, and I had one too many pillows behind my head. Claudia and an unknown man were whispering the corner. A nurse with a heavy accent instructed me to be still.

Claudia came over, and the man and everyone else in the room left. She looked like hell. Tears were flowing when she finally said I had an inoperable brain tumor and had between three to six months to live. She stopped talking, and more tears flowed.

"I can tell you have more to tell me, and it can't get much worse so just spit it out," I said.

"Get ready for this one. Are you ready?" she said.

"You already told me I am dying, so now what? You really don't have the money for this trip, and we are going to jail?"

"You are at least three months pregnant." She pulled up the chair next to the bed, and we laughed and cried together."

"I don't know what to say to any of that." I instinctively wrapped my arms around my belly.

"Your parents will be here in two or three days. I am a little tired. Can't keep flight times straight."

"Where are we?"

"Zurich," Claudia answered

"Switzerland?" I asked.

"Do you know of another one?"

"Wow, I last remember the village. We were going to see the orphanage where Pete spent time. How many days and cities am I missing?"

"No cities, just a few days."

"Will I be able . . . How is the baby?"

"Baby is good and healthy. You had no idea?"

"No. I gained a little bit of weight, but I hadn't been biking all winter. It happens every year. I was tired and worn out but with everything with Pete and the house. I just chalked it up to stress and sadness. I only cut back on drinking because I was dizzy. I was trying to be the rock star travel companion. Some days, I just wanted to sleep."

"You could have said something."

"I am not sleeping away any days in Paris, plus I wanted to be there for you."

"So it was probably morning sickness and not the amazing little bistro in Menton, France that put you down for three days," Claudia said.

"Will I be able to have this baby?"

"The doctors believe so."

"Will you . . ." I wasn't hesitating with the question, only trying to beat the sadness. I knew immediately this is what I wanted. "Will you raise this baby?"

"I would be mad if you didn't ask. It would be my honor."

Doctors and nurses were coming and going all day. Claudia never left my side. In between nurse visits, I laid out some requests. Claudia would call them demands.

That night, I asked, "How did we end up in Zurich?"

"You collapsed in that crappy hotel in the village, then there was a scary ambulance ride to a 'hospital.' Not sure if you ever saw a real doctor. I made alternative plans and got you here. It is one of the best hospitals in the world."

"So I have officially tapped you out of the Pete fund. Is that why you are in my room all the time? You can't afford any other place? Oh man, how are my parents paying for their tickets? Last minute airfare to Europe. Do they even have a valid passport?"

"I got them all set up," Claudia said.

"My mom was not too cool with me spending the Pete fund. There is no way she will accept anything from you. She gave me some money before we left so I wouldn't spend all your money. Mr. and Mrs. Lawrence, my loving parents, have a hard time taking money from others. They don't mind giving it away, but they worked too hard to take from someone else."

"Your dad totally bought the 'I got the travel insurance' line. Told him I doubled down with airline insurance and tour package insurance."

"Oh, he loves checking that box when purchasing airline tickets," I said. "But we are not on any tour?"

"That's right. Doing Europe our way and on our time. Eating our way through every country," Claudia said.

"Damn, I've been eating for two, and now I don't have to worry about gaining weight for bathing suit season."

All night long, we laughed and cried at the inappropriate joke.

"Hey, who was the cutie that was in here? He wasn't in scrubs."

"Sit back and let me tell you about the Pete fund and travel insurance that I call Cade. Literally, I call Cade, and he ensures everything is taken care of. That includes emergency transportation to the best hospital in Europe, two day expedited passports, and more. The Pete fund is a little more than I let on," Claudia said.

When she finally finished, she just looked at me, and together, all we could say was "Hell's bells."

CHAPTER SIXTY

Sherrie speaking here.

Folks, it's still my story . . . I am not gone yet.

Twice, while Claudia was telling me about the Pete fund, the nurse came in because the heart monitor was going crazy. She tried getting Claudia to leave the room, but that only increased my stress level so she was allowed to stay.

The end of my story is close, but I won't get into that. This story and all the others were about my best friend, Claudia, and her move to River Bend. She always triumphed through any adversity. I am proud to say I was along for most of the ride and wouldn't want it any other way.

In one day, I was given a death sentence and the best gift of all. I would not get to meet my baby boy. A month later, I slipped into a coma and was put on life support until my baby could make it on his own.

I insisted on the naming rights for middle and last names. Claudia insisted on the first name since I wasn't allowing it for his last name. The child was meant to be hers, and therefore her last name. I told her to let the people of River Bend assume she had visited the same orphanage where Pete volunteered and that she adopted a child from there. It would explain his darker skin, and some immediate questions would be avoided.

At first, she didn't understand why. Claudia was insisting my boy know me as his mother, and I agreed. It was when she asked about my baby's father she realized I was protecting her from what it meant if he found out he was a dad. The good people of River Bend can assume anything. Claudia will raise Law knowing his family—the Lawrences and Middletons.

My mom and dad are happy with Claudia raising their grandson. The boy's father may figure it out one day, and until then, Claudia will have time and distance from all this sadness to make the right decision and tell him the truth. Oh, if only I could be a fly on the wall the moment Aaron realizes his ex-girlfriend is raising his baby named Lawrence Pete Middleton.

CHAPTER SIXTY-ONE

Claudia's story.

Sherrie better not haunt me since I won't let her have the last word.

She died peacefully in her sleep with her mom, dad, brother, and me at her side. Lawrence was in the NICU for several weeks, and then we stayed for a month before we were able to fly home. Mr. Landin, Cade, and the team at Smith & Madison Title Company took care of the birth certificate and proper paperwork.

Mr. Landin, or his team, had set up that fake news article including a photo of Pete holding a large cardboard check for three hundred thousand dollars. I used this cover story to explain some of the expenses I was paying. My mom and dad believed it too, but in the end, I told both of them the truth about the Pete fund. Don was right about keeping that secret. Everyone needs support. I lost Pete and Sherrie within months of each other. Two great loves of my life but I am able to push forward every day because of the love for my son, Law.

Out of the demands/requests from her deathbed, these are the ones I followed through on. Some because I agreed, and some because I didn't need Sherrie haunting me.

No bike-a-thon. Only one person suggested it, and it was quickly squashed.

Following the service at her parents' church was a large gathering at their home. It was not so must a roast as it was retelling of great stories.

Mia, Jenna, Kay, and I spread some of her ashes on the bike trail near the river and returned to my house. We laughed and cried at all the Sherrie stories. Each one of them begged for their turn tending to Lawrence.

Sherrie and I couldn't agree on which verse I would read, so I simply read both of them at her funeral.

Ecclesiastes 4: 9-10

"Two are better than one because they have a good reward for their toil. For if they fall, one will lift his fellow. But woe to him who is alone when he falls and has not another to lift him!"

Romans 12:9–10

"Let love be genuine. Abhor what is evil; hold fast to what is good. Love one another with brotherly affection. Outdo one another in showing honor."

BOOK CLUB DISCUSSION QUESTIONS

Could you keep winning the lottery a secret?

Does that answer change if you are in your twenties, thirties, or over fifty?

Is there a difference between surprises and secrets?

After finding bones in the basement should Claudia have called the police immediately?

Is hiding the baby's father too big of a secret? Does he have the right to know?

ACKNOWLEDGMENTS

Thank you to my beta readers for the feedback—Alexis, Molly, and Mel. You keep coming through for me—I know it is not an easy read before the edits.

Thank you to my editor, Starr Baumann. The story and mistakes are mine, but Starr helped smooth out the rough edges.

Laci, I appreciate the time you took answering all my tedious medical questions and not giving me a hard time with the liberties I took when bending accuracy to fit the storyline.

Most of all, thank you to my husband, Brian, and son, Alex, for their love and support.

ABOUT THE AUTHOR

After graduating from the University of Wisconsin-Stout, TJ embarked on a career in the hospitality industry, which led to multiple moves across the country. An avid marathon runner, TJ turned to writing after her knee eventually gave out. The author live in Kansas with her husband and son and dog, Reba.